The Many-Coloured Day

THE
MANY-COLOURED
DAY

DAVID MILLS

First published in the United Kingdom in 2008 by
Bank House Books
BIC House,
1 Christopher Road
East Grinstead
West Sussex, RH19 3BT

www.bankhousebooks.com

British Library Cataloguing in Publication Data
A catalogue record for this book is available from the British
Library.

ISBN 9781904408437

Typesetting and origination by Bank House Books
Printed by Lightning Source

To my mother and Rita

I should like to thank all the people who have helped me get this book into print, but most of all I acknowledge the contribution of Gaye King.

Chapter 1

One night in 1763 a carriage raced through the streets of Lichfield, the harness jangling along the horse's back. It was the doctor's carriage and this was no ordinary call.

On the right a turning presented itself and the doctor swung the carriage round. Immediately, framed between the horse's pricked ears, Lichfield Cathedral rose before him. He kept on, passed the cathedral and brought the horse to a stiff-legged halt. Hardly had it stopped before the doctor sprang out, showing a surprising agility for such a big man. He was met at the door and went immediately inside.

Earlier that day Lichfield's other doctor had called at the house and the sick boy within had been *his* patient. This man, Harewood, had done his best, but that afternoon had taken the boy's sister aside. Convinced by the child's failing pulse he had pronounced that her brother would die. He had not done so lightly, and was offended when, by chance, he saw his rival, Sim, take his place.

It was convenient for Harewood that opposite the house in question was the rounded wall of the cathedral's lady chapel. This cast a heavy shadow over the grass, and he hid within it. He watched the lit window of the sickroom avidly: what might be done? The matter was made worse by the boy's father being away; but the child had his sister. His mother was dead.

As Harewood waited the shadow filled the sockets of his eyes, so that a white wink was all that showed. He missed his bed by waiting there but still he waited. What was Sim about? What more was to be done? The longer Harewood waited the more stubborn he became, but Sim did not appear so eventually he was obliged to leave. He had an early start the next day and could not wait indefinitely. When opportunity offered he would enquire after the child, unless he met the undertaker first. Therefore he retired for the night.

Two days later Harewood had opportunity to call upon the boy. He had not met the undertaker and was curious to know what had happened. Wary as he approached the house, he walked with a sombre tread, head down, but at the door he looked up. Beside him, and above, the rectangular windows in their three rows regarded him. There was not the expected funereal air about the place. Harewood's curiosity grew. A minute later he was standing inside the drawing room, impatient, hampered by social niceties.

'Madam,' he said, once he was free to begin his business, 'I have not slept in my anxiety for poor George. I have called lest I was mistaken and his suffering should still continue. Pray, how is the child?'

The woman had been frantic when last they had met; now she was composed and had altogether a different manner. She smiled and directed him to a chair. There was something smug about her, from the doctor's point of view, and she obviously had no intention of hiding this from him. 'I shall show you, Doctor Harewood, by your leave. George. George, come here.'

Harewood heard footsteps on the boards and the child appeared. As if the boy were a ghost the doctor jumped up, glad but with mixed emotions. He could see the alteration in him – but how had Sim done this? George was all wide eyes and pale skin, thin but recovering. In celebrating this moment Harewood swept into a bow and laughed. 'Goodness me, Sir, you are quite a different boy.'

He looked at Miss Wagstaff, meaning to share his pleasure, but noticed only the gloss of her dark hair. She sat with her hands in her lap, her arms white against the yellow of her dress. She had fine, dark brows and these served to make her happiness evident as she looked at him. He almost forgot himself and would gladly have extended this moment, but she looked away.

'The Almighty be praised,' he said, brightly.

'Yes,' she replied, glancing at him. 'And Doctor Sim.'

Harewood stiffened, although he sought not to show it. Miss Wagstaff regretted the remark. 'Indeed,' he said, cheeks rounding. He was irritated, and forgot George until the boy wandered off; but asked if he might call again to ask after his recovery. Miss Wagstaff said that he might.

Harewood took his leave, still brooding (as she surmised) on her remark about Sim. She thought about the two doctors and imagined that she had made some mischief between them, but guessed that it would have come anyway, regardless of her. She watched Harewood as he walked away toward the cathedral, but suddenly George bumped into her and wriggled under her arm. She seemed surprised and smiled, a slow, steady smile, stroking the back of his head before, feeling well satisfied with what she had done, shutting the door on the doctor and his injured feelings.

Chapter 2

Later that day Mr Wagstaff returned and George met him on the drive. Miss Wagstaff, Jenny, joined them and all three linked hands as if they meant to play Ring a Ring o' Roses, laughing and talking at once. Later still Doctor Sim came to call. Whereas Harewood had been young not too long ago, Sim was fresh. Tall, broad, blond, with a russet coat and frills at the sleeves, he brought his freshness in with him as he entered the drawing room. Mr Wagstaff strode up to meet him.

'Give me your hand, Sir!' The old man seemed to struggle for breath. 'I am obliged to you!' The doctor shook hands furiously with Mr Wagstaff, which was farcical, so much did the two men wrestle with each other, but what happened next was telling. As Jenny sometimes said, people reveal themselves in small ways. Sim bent down and beckoned the boy. George reddened, but the doctor drew him on and touched the boy's face with the fingertips of one hand. The moment passed but Sim, realising that they were watching, coloured. Jenny tried to soothe his embarrassment; her father laughed and clapped him on the back.

The doctor was quite good natured about it. He was more interested in something else: he noted Jenny's flinty look to her father; and also that her eyes spoke her thoughts. She frowned under this inspection, but her father, a little man in a wig with a nose like a round doorknob, watched Sim.

4

'My dear sir,' said Wagstaff, who suppressed a smile as Sim seemed to have forgotten him. 'Would you be so kind as to inspect my museum? I should be very grateful for your opinion of it.'

'I should be delighted, Sir!' The handsome young face flushed with pleasure, which communicated itself to those about him. 'Indeed, I have a collection myself of sorts, mostly fossils.'

'Fossils!' Wagstaff grew excited and rubbed his hands, a gesture of which he was quite unconscious.

'Of sea creatures, Mr Wagstaff, shellfish and the like.'

'Sea creatures, George!' said the father to the son, although the frail boy said nothing; his father seemed more animated.

'Might I have the honour of showing you these trifles?' asked Sim. 'Indeed, would you care to display them within your museum?'

'Pray bring them at your earliest convenience,' said Mr Wagstaff. 'Quite the first moment that arises.' He rubbed his hands again. 'Fossils. Left for our wonder, Sir, by the Creator that we may marvel at His works.'

Sim said nothing but found the eyes of Mr Wagstaff and nodded.

'It is a great honour to inspect the museum,' said Miss Wagstaff, smiling and moving with a silken grace toward the door, 'Papa reserves his curiosities for our most prized guests.'

'And such you are and will always be in this house,' said Mr Wagstaff. 'Furthermore, I shall spread your fame among the gentlemen of my acquaintance. You will not go unrewarded.'

Wagstaff took Sim's arm and they walked, new friends, into the rooms where he kept his museum.

Chapter 3

Mr Wagstaff's museum was a wonderful assemblage that was organised, deliberately, in a chaotic way. He had done this partly for impact but also in the hope of creating wonder and thereby glorifying the Creation. So it was that mixed together were all sorts of things, displayed in rows or mounted on the wall, one above another.

In the corner of one room Sim's fossils were now on display. He was proud of his collection and pleased to see it exhibited. Among them were stuffed animals, which he had recommended as oddities but which had a greater significance for him. Among these were two cats with tails of an unusual shape. These were striking and Jenny, as she and Sim toured the museum, drew attention to them.

'How strange the tails are of the two cats.'

She looked back toward them and Sim watched her as she did so. He wondered whether to explain his interest in the cats but was a little distracted. He found his nearness to her a strangely heady thing.

'The shape of the mother's tail is reproduced in the infant,' he said, treading carefully, 'for the kitten was the child of the mother here. Do you not find that curious?'

'No,' she replied, 'We see the same every day. You may observe how my mama in the portrait outside this room

6

exhibits the most striking eyes, features that I believe you may see in George.'

'I noticed them in you,' said Sim, catching her eye for a moment.' Miss Wagstaff reddened. 'But subsequently in the portrait and your brother. What may be the cause of this?'

Jenny looked a moment thoughtful while he stood idly by, one hand rubbing at another. Although she did not realise it he watched her closely. He saw her with his doctor's eyes but those, too, of the man beneath the wig. He noticed the lustre of her hair, and her eyes, with their quickness and winks of humour, drew him, so that he repeatedly returned to them. He decided that it was her brows which made her eyes what they were. Half observing, half enjoying, he noted their jagged turn. Sometimes the doctor in him delighted in such things: young people in the bloom of youth, perfect, who had none of the impairments that came with age. Then they noticed someone outside the window. Doctor Harewood stood there, well dressed and hardly attired for work. It seemed that he had come to visit. Sim and Miss Wagstaff exchanged a glance. They had been enjoying their conversation and did not wish for company, while Harewood, after recognising Sim's carriage, seemed uncertain whether to call.

'Doctor Harewood,' she said.

'Yes,' Sim replied, roguishly. 'I believe that he meant to call on you.'

'How so?' She turned and smiled faintly, raising her eyebrows. Sim opened his mouth to resume their conversation, but Harewood was now staring at Sim's carriage. Perhaps he wondered how a young doctor had come by such a machine – he did not know that it had been a gift from Sim's father – but he was also intrigued by something else. On the door of the carriage Sim had painted the following legend: 'E Mare Omnia', meaning 'Everything From The Sea'. This had only been added in the last few days, and Sim now wondered if it had been altogether wise. Harewood looked at it, then moved off, walking with a purposeful tread, and Sim watched him until he disappeared behind the cathedral.

Finally Sim turned back and Jenny noticed that he now had quite a different look about him. She wanted to know the cause of this change.

'Everything from the sea?' she asked.

The doctor looked at her and saw that he would have to offer some explanation.

'My views about the Creation,' he said, 'are somewhat unconventional.'

Jenny looked at him darkly.

'But I ask you to consider this.' He approached her and she had to raise her face to look at him. 'I am happy to believe,' he said, looking straight into her eyes, 'that the Almighty lies at the root of everything, and so, perhaps, there may not be such a distance between us after all.'

At that point Mr Wagstaff, who had passed round one side of the cathedral while Harewood was on the other, suddenly came upon them. The door opened and he marched in, a bald, brown, wrinkled little man. His blue eyes lit up upon seeing Sim.

'Sim!' he roared, marching over to warmly shake the doctor's hand. 'Had I known you were to come I should not have gone out for a thousand pounds. How d'ye do, Sir?'

'Mr Wagstaff,' said Sim, his smile lighting up his face, the ploughboy cheeks glowing, 'How sorry I was to miss you, and how vexing that you should come now as I was just on the point of leaving. I have a patient to attend, Sir.'

Miss Wagstaff smiled at this untruth. It was a slightly shocking way to treat her father. She had not thought that Sim was about to go. Mr Wagstaff, however, was unaware of this white lie.

'Come again then, Sir, come again.'

Wagstaff graciously steered Sim to the door, but the doctor paused just long enough to take his farewell of Jenny. For a moment their eyes met, and then the door was closed behind him. Jenny watched as he left. She was shocked by his religious views, but what mattered was his belief in the Almighty. Perhaps, as he said, there was not so great a ground between them?

8

Chapter 4

Mr Wagstaff kept his word and wrote to all his acquaintances to recommend Sim. He confided that some of Sim's ideas seemed like 'stuff and nonsense' but recommended him all the same. Among these remarks he promoted Sim's work in education. The doctor had a name in this field, but did not tell Mr Wagstaff how the interest arose. To be frank, Sim had fathered a daughter with a servant. He regretted his weakness, but the child was his and Sim supported her; indeed he loved her. When convenient he intended to bring her to Lichfield. For the moment he said nothing of her, nor mentioned her in the sketch that he provided to Wagstaff of his life.

Soon after saving George, whether it was thanks to Mr Wagstaff or not, Sim received a most unusual letter. He opened this halfway up his stairs, a position made glorious by the cathedral behind his home, but the letter quickly distracted him from any thought of the view outside.

> My Dear Sir,
>
> I have lately had the advantage of being introduced to your ideas regarding the education of females and am most anxious to meet with you to discuss them.
>
> On Friday of this week I shall be at the Blue Boar to dispute a point of honour with a gentleman whose conduct

has obliged me to challenge him. Might I request your attendance, at eight in the morning, when your medical skills may well be called upon, although I do assure you, Sir, that there will be no sword or gun play. I merely intend to beat him into a better way of thinking.

When the affair is concluded, and should all be well, I hope to speak with you with regard to a most pressing educational matter.

I am, Sir, most respectfully,
Thomas Bagshaw

Sim gave out a puff of air and thought a moment. He did not approve of duels. He could not help but wonder, too, about a man who conducted business on a duelling ground. Despite this he was curious, and determined to make himself available if he possibly might.

That Bagshaw had heard of Sim was pleasing to the doctor, but the wonder was that Sim had not yet heard of him. Mr Bagshaw was well enough known around his estate. In truth, his estate workers marvelled at him: Mr Bagshaw was good-hearted, although no-one's fool – but unusual. For example, when George Lee got soused and missed his turn at the harvest, Bagshaw fetched him, dragged him out and doused him in the yard. Normally, though, he was more restrained. It was also true that when illness affected his workers or young people abandoned the land and left parents in dependence and want, then he was always sympathetic.

When Sim arrived at the Blue Boar Inn on the morning of the duel he was surprised by the number of people who were there, all along the side of the inn as far as the duelling ground, along the rutted cart track that led to the fields.

The doctor was uncomfortable among these people who did not know him. Some of them left their eyes on him longer than he liked. He saw them measure his worth, but he was a proud man and would not be cowed. In fact he turned his attention to the crowd and tried to make sense of the congestion. Among the many he began to pick out the principals, among whom he thought he detected his correspondent.

In particular Sim noticed three men. One stood next to a horse. The animal's haunches shone with a coppery burnish, and the fellow draped a hand over them. Two daft cronies sat, still mounted, behind. These men were like monkeys in fashionable rig; but the first one, what might one say of him? He drew the eye. He generated a sense of something, something unpleasant, as well as manifesting a sort of country bull masculinity. This was Smart, Bagshaw's opponent. While waiting, he glowered and breathed through his nose with great draughts, seeming hardly able to contain himself.

It was now that Sim paid his first attention to Mr Bagshaw. Bagshaw was a big man, heavy and with broad shoulders, which were stooped. Only twenty-two, he had a face that bore the marks of a pox. In compensation for this he had fine eyes, if dreamy. His cheeks were large and pendulous. He was clearly clean, and Sim was struck that he was dressed without the least regard to fashion.

Mr Bagshaw seemed to observe the horsemen as an interesting but despicable species. This evident distaste drew forward the man who had lent upon the horse. He came up and filled that space, close about Bagshaw, which no-one should have intruded upon. Indeed, Bagshaw could see nothing else. Bagshaw felt all the unpleasantness of Smart's crooked face but what most disgusted him was the gentleman's rig upon such a rascal: pig-tailed hair, green waistcoat, buckskin breeches, and white stockings from his knees down to his boots. It was time they had done.

'Have you a supporter, Sir, among this rabble?'

In saying this a spark came into Smart's eyes which caught the light in the way a glaucoma might. Bagshaw quietly admitted that he had no second. This brought one of Smart's companions forward, and only then was Bagshaw separated from Smart – who stepped aside so that Bagshaw might choose a weapon. His companion aped a civility: an extraordinary thing, it seemed, to Bagshaw. The man was dressed as a gentleman but was clearly a lout. Consequently Bagshaw ignored him, and his pistols. Consequently too the man spat at Bagshaw, who winced noticeably but retained his discipline.

Alone in the midst of this Bagshaw felt a great strain, and people noticed his reluctance to choose a weapon. His indecision set the crowd in motion and a low conversation started. Sim was suddenly sorry for him. So much weight seemed to have found its way upon him and, in truth, Bagshaw took a step backwards and looked about him, ran his eyes for a moment among the many, who were mostly familiar to him. Those who, ordinarily, would have been deferential now met his eyes with a hard, market day sort of look, like that of buyers at a stock ring.

In no way, no visible way, did the outward aspect of Bagshaw alter, but it was enough. The knot that had seemed sealed now broke up and a loose disunity set in. In view of their being disappointed many might have repaired to the inn, but a promise of what might now be done to their fallen champion kept them there. The man with the guns, done with civility, broke out in a raucous vulgarity. "Oose got no spurs? A fine cock 'e is!'

The other two men, in quite ridiculous response to this, threw back their heads and roared. The men were at liberty now, as they imagined; they meant to beat Bagshaw. Smart threw off his waistcoat, and any semblance of the gentleman. He spoke to Bagshaw in the most graphic terms, and Bagshaw blanched, it must be said, as Smart postured and the men crowded round him. Sim could not help but feel Bagshaw's loneliness. The doctor's hand grew red on the handle of his bag.

'Sir.' Bagshaw's voice had a modicum of emotion but he held himself in check, his back very straight. 'As I made clear in my letter it is not my desire to kill you nor, I may say in perfect candour, to be killed; rather it is my intention, as you will recall, to engage you in boxing and to thrash you until you recant the tenets of your reprobate life. To your mettle, Sir.'

The three men were confused at this. Bagshaw began to prepare himself for a boxing match.

'No, pistols!'

'To your mettle, Sir!'

Smart stood uncertain. What, however, might he do? He stood sourly a moment, a moment for thought, and then he began to gesture the people back. A loosely formed square was made and he, now, was a trifle uncertain. The eyes now shifted to him. He was an excellent shot, even after taking alcohol.

'Pistols' he said, 'or we thrash you.'

He took the pistols again and shoved one at Bagshaw, who refused it. He did this as if he thought the thing was dirty.

'You may shoot me,' he said in his distaste for the weapon, 'if you have a mind to, but daresay you will hang for it; and come, Sir, have you so little regard for yourself that you require these rascals to defeat me? No, Sir, to your mark.'

In the saying of these words it became clear that conversation was at an end; it also became clear that Bagshaw had had some schooling at fisticuffs. He held up his fists, with his forearms at right angles to his upper arms; with his legs braced he padded round. Further, and most appropriately, he adopted a fearsome scowl and raised his bottom lip like a bulldog's. Smart, in the next moment, dived beneath him. This dirty trick set the tone for the rest of the combat. Smart quite smothered Bagshaw and got in a very telling blow between his legs, where Bagshaw, despite his breeding, was still vulnerable: indeed, he let out several panting cries. All the while he could do nothing but fend Smart off as he, still on top of him, made repeated wild swings.

'You rascal, Sir!' managed Bagshaw.

'Blackguard, blackguard, blackguard!' shouted Smart with each wild assault.

Smart grabbed hold of Bagshaw's hair and tugged violently, so Bagshaw's head shook; the best efforts of Bagshaw to prevent this only led to Smart biting him on the wrist. And so the fight continued.

At length, and having been severely bitten, the underdog managed to gain the advantage. One moment Smart was flailing like a mad man, the next a solid, square fist smacked onto his chin. The squire sagged and straightway slumped from his seat.

Bagshaw got up and made some attempt at brushing the dirt from him, paying great attention to some dung in which he had been rolled. Smart, meanwhile, was on his knees.

'Well, Sir,' asked Bagshaw, when a bloodied, dirtied squire got to his feet. 'Will you concede and agree to make reparation, or would you go on?'

Smart thought, but in the main only to recover his breath. He would go on.

For him a life of late nights and short days, which was not that of a fighting man, began to tell. However, waving away his cronies, he sought to find the measure of Bagshaw. He charged him, his head down, fists arching towards Bagshaw's face; he sought to outbox him and the two moved round like Easter hares; he sought again to overturn him; he tried to kick but, through it all, Bagshaw moved stiffly, blocked and parried and, though with less force and moderated frequency, struck the squire with telling blows. This went on until, before long, Smart was in no condition to continue.

'Enough, Sir,' said Bagshaw. 'Will you make some reparation to Miss Mary Evans?'

Smart made no answer but charged like a mad thing. Bagshaw dropped him on their first contact. The squire sank first to his knees then collapsed onto his front.

'Enough, Sir!'

Bagshaw spoke, and with a noticeable degree of emotion in his voice. His big face was trained to dissemble from showing any pain, but his eyes (which were admittedly much to be noticed) were lambent and full of pity. 'Will you give it up, Sir? Will you not undertake to provide for this unfortunate lady?'

'I will not.'

Smart staggered wearily, but got to his feet. One of his eyes was closing fast and his bottom lip looked as if it was inside out. All the muck and mud, the blood – of Bagshaw as well as his own – the damage to his clothing, the hurt to his hair, made his condition seem infinitely worse than it was. His exhaustion, however, was real enough; but the man again got his fists up.

'Then I must provide for her.' Bagshaw shook his head, adopting another tone and speaking in his mellow, baritone voice. He looked, too, toward Smart with a sort of rueful affection. The eyes became kind and the round flap cheeks drew into a smile. 'You are a brave man, Sir, even if you are a rascal.'

Smart grunted. After a moment of what looked like emotion, perhaps shame, he began to collect his scrambled thoughts. 'You could not break me.'

'No,' said Bagshaw. 'I could not break you.'

Now came the strangest thing. Smart, catching Bagshaw's eye, nodded. There was a moment of respect between them. Sim saw this, fascinated. Indeed, the other men would have beaten Bagshaw, but Smart called them to heel. Within a minute they had ridden through the crowd and gone. Their horses left hoof prints in the mud but there was nothing else left of them; and so the episode ended. It ended, that is, in its essentials. This was the greater part but only a part. The many eyes were still turned on Bagshaw, and it took great will not to show the relief that now overcame him, which he embraced as a holy thing; a cross borne to Calvary when the spirit was weak.

'Pardon me, Sir. I am Doctor Sim.'

Sim's voice drew Bagshaw from himself. Bagshaw turned and, very civilly, greeted the doctor. For his part Sim was glad to shake Bagshaw's hand. He now knew from talk among the crowd that Smart had left a woman from Bagshaw's estate in child, without thought of behaving well toward her; hence Bagshaw had protected her in the manner that he had.

For a moment the two men looked at one another. They were on an similar footing in build and each was above six foot two; Sim more regular in his face, but Bagshaw more flabby and heavier in his build, which was less athletic than Sim but greater in tonnage.

Suddenly Bagshaw became animated.

'My dear Sir, I live alone and have a retired life. My ways are not those of the world. I despise vanity, frippery, and yet all around me am vexed to find it. I have an idea, Sir. I believe that children, if taught the best principles, may grow without vice; that people, raised by reason, taught to despise all that is false, may prize only virtue.'

Sim smiled. Such was the enthusiasm of Bagshaw that he felt all the sincerity of the young man.

'Women,' said Bagshaw suddenly, somewhat warily. He glanced to the side then went on. 'Like men, I grant you, are often spoiled in their rearing. Our women of fashion are decorative, farmers of compliments, like dogs trained to dance, brought up from a young age to please men. But ought not a woman, Sir, be educated according to her potential? Should a wife be a helpmeet rather than a hand-maid?

Sim gave this some thought and was receptive.

'I live alone,' said Bagshaw, 'and my thoughts have lately turned towards finding a wife. Here I must confide in you. I hope that I may trust your discretion?' Sim was near affronted. Some trace of this must have been evident to Bagshaw who, by a sudden gesture, waved away the offence. None the less, the same expression also served as an apology. Bagshaw then dropped his voice and spoke softly as he gazed into Sim's eyes. 'I have lately

15

been disappointed in love, rejected for the third time and find that I have little in common with young ladies of fashion. I am also convinced that were such a woman to accept me there could be no satisfaction in the match. I have, therefore, determined to adopt a girl, raise her with strict regard to the best educational principles and marry her once she becomes of sufficient age.'

Sim was a young man but he was seldom surprised by anything; however, he said nothing for a rather long moment, at least nothing in words. Bagshaw watched him.

'I require you to help me choose a fine, healthy girl and one likely to be receptive.' He frowned and caught the doctor's eyes. 'I, too, am a man who may be trusted, Doctor Sim.'

Sim considered this. It was a serious matter, and the doctor made no attempt to hide the thought that he was giving it. The matter turned like water round a mill wheel behind his eyes, although he was quite satisfied of Bagshaw's trustworthiness.

'Yes,' said the doctor. 'I know that, Mr Bagshaw. I have no doubt of it at all.'

'I thank you, Sir,' replied Bagshaw.

'However,' said Sim. Bagshaw frowned again but Sim went on undeterred. 'Sir, forgive me, but may I recommend to your acquaintance a woman known to me, a friend of mine, whom I know to be searching for a partner in life? She is young, amiable, pleasing in her person, well educated, possessed of a large estate and has a mind, I venture to suggest, not unlike your own. Will you consent, Sir, at least to meet her before you begin upon this scheme?'

Bagshaw was sufficiently polite to consider what was said to him. His mind, however, had a great tenacity; furthermore he was somewhat affronted. 'Thank you, Sir, but I know not how you, having just met me, may recommend to me a wife. I think it better that I select my own.'

Sim did not care for this answer; the two men were not entirely comfortable for a moment. They grew silent and Sim thought about the matter carefully. There could not be one chance in a million of the scheme ever reaching fruition; however, some good might come from rescuing a child from an orphanage, and of Bagshaw's integrity he had no doubt; therefore he agreed. At once the enthusiasm returned into Bagshaw's eyes, which were very white against all the dirt on his pear-shaped face.

'I have arranged to travel to an orphanage. Perhaps you would help me in selecting a girl? Once I have done this I shall move my home to Lichfield to be near your help and advice.'

The doctor was again a little surprised, but Mr Bagshaw extended a hand toward him. Sim looked at it a moment, shook it and the arrangement was sealed. He would travel with Bagshaw to help him select a wife.

Chapter 5

The coachman hauled on the reins and the horses came to a jangling halt. At the same time the principal of the orphanage came running out. The coach settled on its undercarriage and Sim and Mr Bagshaw descended.

'Mr Bagshaw?' asked the principal. Bagshaw came forward and then introduced Sim. The man was civil to Sim but his interest was in Bagshaw. This was to be expected, but Sim smiled that the man looked so hard, as he seemed to think himself subtle in it. He simpered round them and feted them, but how he watched. He continued to do this as he led them into the building. He was a bent little thin man, his cheeks permeated by red and blue, but with acute eyes. Bagshaw felt himself to be on trial, and this was well.

The man led them under the arched doorway into the dark and Spartan interior. In the entry hall was a wooden staircase, and the man, whose name was Bates, led them up it. Nowhere was there any indication of children, but there was a smell, part clean and part not, the dirty part of which was that of human animals.

At the top of the first flight they were directed into a room. The man installed them in chairs and took a seat that faced them. The room was walled with books. In a cabinet were the ledgers of the orphanage, which moved Bagshaw – as so many young lives were bound in it. He wondered how many children passed through this place, a responsibility that, he thought, might be read in Bates.

'Well, Mr Bagshaw,' said Bates at last. 'You want to raise one of my girls?'

'That is correct.'

'You have testimonials?'

'I have.'

Bagshaw produced his references in a flourish from under his coat. Bates delayed in taking them; perhaps he implied that nothing would be done in haste. At last, however, he took them and went to the better light of the window, where he began to hum to himself. This grew loud, and he rocked on his heels, but at length he regained his seat – to state firmly that he was assured of Bagshaw's integrity. Bagshaw bowed and Bates did the same, but began to question him. Did he understand the burden he was undertaking? Were his motives sound? Would he tire of his responsibility?

The doctor listened, knowing that nothing would dissuade Bagshaw and that the man wasted his breath. Nevertheless, it was well to ask these questions once more. He had asked them himself, more than once.

Bagshaw sat very still and rested his eyes heavily on Mr Bates. He met the enquiries with good humour, save once when Bates became rather too paternalistic. Even though Bagshaw would not be patronised, this only ruffled him – and the old man soon ran out of enquiries. Before the child was chosen from the company, Bates approached Bagshaw. He looked a bent old thing but he eyed the young man keenly. Much was conveyed and much understood, but Bagshaw did not resent this. He was a man of his word, but Bates was not to know. Suddenly Bagshaw jumped up.

'Give me your hand, Sir. So many must the children be hereabouts, in desperate circumstances, and so great must the pressure be upon space and resources in your establishment, that it would be easy for you to wish one of them away; yet you do not forego any of your charges lightly and I respect you for it.'

Mr Bates seemed surprised, a little embarrassed, but he returned, none the less, to one last perusal of the documentation. Plainly Bates did not like the business. This, however, was of no consequence. At length he seemed to realise that there might be no more delay, and went to the door.

'Mrs Collins.'

Bates studied them, somewhat subdued but nevertheless reconciled and suddenly impatient. Again he called Mrs Collins. This time a middle-aged woman appeared. Like Mr Bates she was dressed in second-hand clothes, in her case a homespun gown with calico facings. Like Bates, too, she looked worn out.

'Be so good,' said Bates, 'as to line up the girls outside.'

The door closed behind her and they heard her on the stairs. Other adult voices suddenly reached them – always stern – and then came a tramp, a tramp-tramp-tramp, and the voices of children, girls without question. The stairs creaked: tramp, tramp, tramp.

Bagshaw sat through this, calm and serious, his eyes perhaps enlivened by some spark, but very still. For Sim, so much energy upon the stairs was pleasing. He sat keenly on the edge of his seat, also diverted by the faces of the two men: the calm of Bagshaw; the fretful resolution in the thin face of Bates.

Bates, after a minute or two, perhaps more, got to his feet and the gentlemen were invited to accompany him outside. Their tramp sounded upon the stairs.

In the light of the wide outdoors, both men squinted. It was a moment before they were possessed of themselves. Before them, as they began to focus with clarity, they saw rows of children.

This moment, the crux of their visit, was something of a shock. The reaction of the girls to them was marked – shock. Sim, as he would be, was a watcher of people. It was not remarkable that he detected the anxiety, for example, that Bates felt in this business, but he also managed to see something of Bagshaw's real feelings. It seemed to Sim that Bagshaw disliked this himself. There was something of the stock ring about it and Bagshaw seemed aware of this. As Sim often was (although this was not always the case), he was right and Bagshaw did feel uncomfortable. He hated to give anything of himself away, but smiled in pity at so many unwanted children. Both he and Sim also noticed how thin they were: food must be rationed. He noted, too – although with ambivalence, as he believed in work and disliked finery – their coarse clothing. He knew that this was a uniform, since the girls were required to work, but he wondered how many hours they spent in these clothes.

'Poor creatures.'

Sim turned at Bagshaw's remark but said nothing, and then looked again to the girls and ran his eye over them. This was another of his tricks; he had learnt to deduce all sorts of things. He wondered about the hard eyes that some of these children had: what could have given them such wariness, even cynicism? He could see other things too, like malnutrition, and a look that he had learned to associate with consumption. Sim was quite affected, Bagshaw more collected; or, at least, he pretended this.

Suddenly Bagshaw made a start. The massed ranks of girls almost baulked under his approach. One after another the eyes of each child widened into his along the front row. The second line he inspected in the same way; the third, the fourth, the fifth.

'My dear,' said Bagshaw, stopping occasionally, 'who is the King?' This he asked by way of a test. Other questions also occurred to him, but to his first question the answers were various.

'You, Sir?' stammered one blonde and evidently terrified child; 'Mr Bates?' said another; 'George the Third,' announced a third.

This child positively bloomed on being told that she was right. She had the most charming brown eyes, and her eyebrows were remarkably fine, seemingly picked out, in definite purpose, by the brush of Romney or Wright. Oh, but how her face changed when she realised that being correct might condemn her. She only looked, with wide and anxious eyes, upon being asked a further question. Furthermore, the attention of the second gentleman, who came and stood behind the first, oppressed her, for all the winning tone that he adopted in his unregistered talk with her.

It was with palpable relief that at last the moment of trial passed from her. At last her tormentors moved off. Sim could not help but laugh in seeing the poor creature relax. She was at once restored to her prettiness and interest in the proceedings. She even found Sim's eyes, which smiled for her.

Once again, as before, sunk in thought, stopping here and there and putting questions, predicting growth, as the doctor had instructed him, eyeing, probing, questioning, Bagshaw went round the group, and other children were subjected to his individual attention. In their turn these children were treated to the recompense of Sim, the kindly and innocuous comments that followed the horse-fair ministrations of his friend. Then, evidently, a decision was made. In consideration of his interest Bagshaw told Sim. The company, three hundred eyes, watched, each trying to gauge Sim's reaction. They saw the news register. The tall, handsome man with the kind words was wily enough, though, to keep the intelligence to himself. The two moved to the front, before the ranks, where Bates and Mrs Collins stood by. Once again there was a conversation. Unlike Sim, however, Mrs Collins did look and one half of the girls knew themselves to be safe.

None the less one little girl began to shudder, justifiably. Bates and Mrs Collins and the men began to move. In breathless suspense the pretty, brown-eyed girl watched them as they approached her. No-one else near had been questioned, but she hoped, watching for their interest to take them elsewhere. They came on. Mrs Collins, indeed, had her eyes on her; the other adults stared; the girls all stared; and a burst of loud conversation was quelled. They were all looking at her now. The girl trembled; she did not want to go. Barely was she able to understand Mrs Collins, who put her face very near hers and whispered some comfort: she was to be educated; she was to live in a big house; she was to become a lady.

'Ah doh' want educatin'!' she shouted, her eyes blazing one moment into those of this large man – bigger than Mr Bates or even Wink, who brought the coal – and who waited, evidently, for her to become composed; which she could not be. Mr Bates put his arm round her and the girl at last, who had not wanted to, began crying. Big, rolling tears coursed down her cheeks and her mouth, so nice and soft, became twisted.

Sim stood back. He did not care for this. He felt a sense of distaste and had to remind himself of the good that they did there. For two pins he would have urged Bagshaw to give up. Bates, too, and Mrs Collins were also sorely troubled, but Bagshaw remained calm. It was not true to say that he was unmoved, as he was flushed; never had Sim seen him so far drop his languid, controlled self. Bagshaw was also full about his eyes, but he was determined and the child had to go.

The note of the girl rose above their voices as they began, in haste, towards the coach, but she had to go. Henceforward she was helped the sixty or so yards that remained. At the coach Mrs Collins stooped, hugging the child to her. Bates, too, clasped himself to the girl, and then she clung to one after the other until she was put inside.

Someone ran up, and a few things were put in through a window. Bates fixed his eyes on Bagshaw and recalled the terms and exactness of their agreement, to which Bagshaw nodded; and then the coach began to roll, the little thing sitting upright in the window as they left the yard and remaining so while the house was visible. Thereafter she sank slowly under the ministrations of the men into a corner, and cried softly.

Chapter 6

Before the carriage reached Lichfield the child had ceased crying, though she continued miserable. Bagshaw, shocked, had to remind himself that she could not yet be expected to be rational. Sim, with more experience of children, more easily appreciated this fact.

It had been Sim who had talked the girl from the worst of her upset. Bagshaw, while willing, had not been adept; stiff and grave as he was, he had not yet learned the right pitch in speaking to her.

For all this he was a man who became more agreeable with acquaintance, although Sim, conversely, had the knack of instantly pleasing. For example, a handkerchief served in a number of conjuring tricks and he made a penny vanish, as it seemed, and other things of this sort. Bagshaw (while not permitting it to undermine his own sense of worth) almost envied his friend's capacity to please. Before they reached Lichfield Sim and the girl had a tolerable friendship.

Their approach brought them down into the city, riding along a rutted road. For some way the cathedral had been visible and they competed to look at it. At one point three heads poked from the carriage.

The coach now turned from the main highway, away from the city, but there was still traffic on the road and there were people along the pavements. Once or twice the doctor was recognised or made recognitions. Bagshaw noticed that some of the people to whom he spoke were obviously poor.

The long way about took them round the city, and they seemed to leave Lichfield on their right; but a minute or so saw them approach Stowe Pool and a church. The church tower was a marker, and within a minute they had arrived at the house that Bagshaw had rented. This was smart: high shouldered, red brick, with white dressings around the windows and the corners of the walls.

When the carriage came to a halt the three of them sat a moment while the last of the momentum left them. The carriage grew still, a shadow approached and the door was opened for them. The outside day rushed in but for a second they remained. The realisation that the great enterprise had begun was a shocking one. Then Sim, Bagshaw and Fanny, as she had been renamed, to her consternation, got out and, having collected one or two things, walked to the door and went inside.

That afternoon, at six, the girl sat on a chair in the smart and expansive drawing room, amazed at her liberty. She waited for the doctor who had promised to come after six. Usually she would have been coming to the end of her day's work, and she envied her friends their labour. She missed them and, as she thought, her recollection brought a smile to her cheeks, quite different to her mood; but she was composed.

Behind her brown and sparkling eyes she was now with Betty and Annie and Mary and Floss, and Mr Bates was coming round and they were pretending to be busy. None the less, there was an interest, way behind her eyes, in the prospect of the city. Mr Bagshaw had said that they would go tomorrow to Lichfield. She was to have clothes and shoes. Again, however, Bagshaw had frightened her. She was not to hanker after luxuries. Fanny had never met these temptations, and was terrified lest her evident wickedness overpower her.

She glanced to look at her protector, Bagshaw, who was bent at a wide, glossy table. Fanny was shocked that he had a double chin, seated as he was. With his brows down for concentration, his mouth all pushed up, he was most frightful.

As she glanced round the room she steadily began to grow familiar with her surroundings. She had never known a carpet before, and the gloss of the furniture amazed her. Quite obviously Mr Bagshaw was very rich. She also noticed the bookcases that stood along two walls. The spines of the books intrigued her, as did the windows. Fanny was interested by the size of the garden, and there were trees along the windows whose topmost branches tapped at the glass above. Past the trees and the lawn was the road that had brought her and still might take her back. Beyond that was an expanse of water and beyond that, though she saw it more in her mind's eye, was all the muddle of the town, all the many roofs, in such an array. But the cathedral, as Mr Bagshaw called it, was most compelling – the spires so enormous, and three of them!

As Fanny sat there, waiting, the sense began to grow in her that the day was drawing to a close, and this began to make her feel miserable. A sense, a sense she tried to fight but gradually overcame her, gnawed at her, saying that if she went now, if they would take her, perhaps if she ran, she might return home, be reinstated, before the night came and overtook her and trapped her here.

The quiet sobbing of the girl drew the attention of Bagshaw, and of a sudden she was surprised to feel his hands upon her. Fanny jumped and cried all the louder, but he took her up. She was beaten, and he carried her off to the chair from which he had come, arranging her, rather like a bag he had to carry on a carriage journey.

Fanny was now so frightened that she trembled. Bagshaw laughed, seeing that he was such a monster, but he spoke to her and she found that he had a nice voice. He began upon something, and was talking to her in his stern but rather gentle way when a knock sounded upon the door. It was the manservant, Bingley.

'Doctor Sim, Sir, and Miss Wagstaff.'

Bingley went out and Sim soon came in. He was pink-faced and smart, in a russet brown suit, white stockings and a bushy wig, which was absurd beside his youth. He entered smiling and introduced to them a striking young woman: dark, with quick, kind eyes and a mouth turned a fraction at the ends. Bagshaw was unsettled and Fanny, who was quick, noticed him blush, and that he and the doctor exchanged glances.

In truth Bagshaw was cross. He had expected Sim, no-one else. There was a moment when he considered being

26

disagreeable. Sim saw this and offered apology, but deftly, so that the woman was not embarrassed, and Bagshaw, showing that he was not ill-bred, contrived to avoid a scene. However, his recognition of his guests was little more than civil, which Fanny noticed was not lost upon the young woman.

In fact, little escaped Fanny and she saw that the woman, Miss Wagstaff, was not an easy mix with Mr Bagshaw. She noted, too, that the doctor seemed happier in her company. Sim was attentive to her, whereas Bagshaw seemed ill at ease. Had she known it, Bagshaw was horrified by the woman's clothing. For example, her yellow silk dress had a full skirt and tight bodice – shocking, although it suited her. It showed her arms and all the white length of them was exposed below the elbow; it also had a superfluous flounce at the elbows. Worse than this flounce was something else: the dress had a low neckline, thinly veiled by a gauze handkerchief.

Fanny watched them until she was introduced, when, to her fury, she blushed and was hardly able to answer for herself. For the first time she was aware of her Staffordshire accent, when these people had no accent between them. But the woman waited without seeming to wait and, eventually, Fanny took heart enough to look up and was met by two most lovely eyes. Miss Wagstaff saw that she had been crying, took some water and with a handkerchief wiped at Fanny, making a great show of concentration to draw attention from the girl. She achieved this – both men watched her – but Fanny, despite herself, was also absorbed. She looked at the woman's eyes from chin down and chin up, full on and glancing sideways, and greatly admired their arresting quality. She also approved of the gloss of her black/brown hair, which (had Fanny known it) she might have likened to a Newmarket filly.

'I beg you, Madam,' said Mr Bagshaw, 'not to mollycoddle the girl. She is to have the hardiness of a Spartan.'

Mr Bagshaw frowned and rocked on his heels, but Sim smiled. He did this slyly, removed from them, standing by the fireplace. Bagshaw was annoyed, brows down, mouth screwed up, and Miss Wagstaff, in between maintaining what was proper, flickered at the corners of her mouth, and her eyes narrowed.

'Come, Sir, she is what, ten years old?'

In defiance she gathered Fanny up and Fanny, in disregard of Bagshaw, nestled against the firm but giving shape of Miss Wagstaff at the chest. The men watched and the moment between the woman and child drew out, becoming private, excluding Sim and the impatience of Bagshaw alike. The doctor knew that the girl's clothing was unclean, but the woman rocked her. Suddenly Fanny chanced the woman's eyes and Miss Wagstaff smiled, a smile that might have toasted the men's muffins. However, Miss Wagstaff was not unmindful of the strange Mr Bagshaw. At length she put Fanny down but detained her for a moment.

'You and I shall be great friends,' she said. 'Remember, Sir,' she said, turning to Bagshaw suddenly, more crisp in her manner, 'when you were first taken from your home and sent away to school. Can you recall how unhappy you were?'

'There is a great deal of unhappiness, Madam, in life,' replied Bagshaw, puffing out his cheeks and dropping his chin, which greatly increased his gravitas, 'and it is well that we learn how to live with it.'

Bagshaw said this as if he were addressing a public meeting. He raised his eyebrows and waited for a riposte, but Sim, who knew women better than his friend, noticed the reply she made. The woman's eyes narrowed a moment and there was a flicker of winter in her greeny brown eyes. This was lost upon Bagshaw. He gave a nod of satisfaction at her silence, and made the unwitting gesture of tilting his head in the contemplation of his victory, still rocking on his heels. Sim smiled as the cold eyes swept over Bagshaw again.

Tea was brought and the child was encouraged to help administer it. She had never had tea, nor met so dainty a teapot or such small cups as she was instructed to fill. This task she managed very prettily, and Bagshaw thanked her gravely, but the girl was showing signs of tiredness and he was not slow to realise this. He got up, under the observation of the others.

'Come, Fanny.'

The child offered her hands and Bagshaw eased her up. She was confused but was learning to give herself up. Moreover she was more trusting now with her protector. Bagshaw bent down and the child was encouraged to bend on her knees, facing him.

'Oh Father,' he began, 'grant us safe lodging this night and a holy rest.' This said he smiled and returning, quite unabashed, to the company, rang the bell for Bingley.

'Say goodnight to our company,' said Bagshaw, in his stiff, kind way, and the child turned her eyes on them all and made a little curtsey. At this there was a great laugh. Poor Fanny – but Miss Wagstaff extended a consoling arm toward her and Bagshaw was kind, although he also noticed Miss Wagstaff's plump white arm. Next Sim came up. Like a grandee he dismissed Fanny, but did not embarrass her, and the girl was thus sent to her bed.

When the child was gone the adults fell to a breezy, adult conversation about her; at least Sim and Miss Wagstaff did, but Bagshaw did not want to say much. He would keep his confidence for a longer and surer acquaintance with her. The conversation therefore quickly took another turn. They spoke of medicine and then of London. Bagshaw said that he preferred to be 'out of the stink of metropolitan living'. They spoke of this and that. During this conversation Miss Wagstaff spoke her mind with clarity and precision. Despite this, Bagshaw sometimes pooh-poohed her. Sim noticed however how quick she was to grasp complex principles of engineering, a subject that left Bagshaw bored. He also noticed how perverse she was in continuing to discuss them, despite Bagshaw's boredom.

These conversations, however, were but passing. The girl had not long been gone when the doctor rose, claiming an early start on the morrow, and Miss Wagstaff, who had happened to meet Sim on her evening walk, got up to leave with him, for decency's sake, and because her father might by now be wondering where she was. Thus it was that Bagshaw took a civil leave of Miss Wagstaff and she a civil leave of him, and Sim stood watching them. Thereafter he shook Bagshaw's hand and the door closed behind them.

Once they were gone Bagshaw retired to a chair. The light was fading now outside but the last of it seeped into the room and fell across his face as he draped himself, inelegantly, near the hearth. Something of his deep thought could be seen in his expression. Once or twice he muttered something, but there was no-one there to hear him, and finally he got up and went to bed.

Chapter 7

The house where Sim lived was a fine house. It was built of red brick, with arched windows dressed in white stone. Over the door was a portico, also of stone, and from the door to the street spanned a bridge across the old moat. The house boldly asserted Sim's promise, but for all his talent he had no patient to visit that morning, no paying patient. He had been out on a charitable call, but such calls would not pay his bills and he must have paying patients.

In the ditch below lilacs and roses had been planted, and there were also apple trees which now were dressed in pink. The sky above was blue and the roads were drying, making passage easier. This fact, which should have pleased him, chafed: he should be on the road himself.

Sim pressed his face to the glass and could just discern his broad forehead, with the tapered shape of his face. There was something too showing of the white about his eyes. He pondered his reflection, but soon looked through it into the road.

He began to think of a system of shorthand that he was devising. He had so many ideas that a shorthand method would be valuable. As his thoughts roamed onward he was distracted by movement in the road. Unexpectedly, Doctor Harewood was calling upon him. Sim expected a summons, but Harewood soon retreated and Sim heard a servant on the stairs. There came a knock, the door opened and Taplin, lank, dour hound as he was, appeared in the doorway.

'What is it, Mr Taplin?

'A note, Sir.'

Sim stamped over from the window and snatched it, just managing to thank Taplin before dismissing him. He was curious and returned to the window in haste, opening the letter as he went.

Sir,

I have thought it proper to tell you that your patient, Mr Gittus, of Field Mill, Shenstone, has asked me to relieve you of your care of him. Likewise Mr Thompson of Loxley, Staffordshire, has also returned to me. Finally (for the present) I must also report that Mr Swan has returned to my care and I venture to suggest – you will of course rejoice in this – seems likely to be restored to full health under my supervision.

I am Sir, your most humble servant,
Doctor Elias Harewood.

'Confound the man!' snorted Sim.

He crumpled the note in a grinding and prolonged action and threw it down. For a moment he thought about seeking out the good doctor and asking how he had acquired so many of his patients. He sat and pondered this, one hand upon a knee while he stroked under his nose with his other hand. His decision to confront Harewood came suddenly upon him. If he were quick he might catch him. Sim clattered over the boards and a moment later was on the stairs.

Harewood's house (smaller than Sim's) was opposite the entrance to the Close, just a few yards away. Sim was soon across the dirty street and, in a moment more, approached Harewood's door. However, about this time he began to collect himself. This was not through apprehension, but by a sense of what was becoming. His knock upon the door was, consequently, more genteel than it might have been.

To Sim's surprise, Harewood answered the door himself. This was a moment before Sim was ready, and he found himself caught between good manners and the wish to be disagreeable.

The two men looked at each other and Harewood, rather pointedly, waited for Sim to state his business.

'I am obliged to you, Sir,' said Sim at length, 'for the note that you were good enough to bring me.'

Harewood inclined his head, and augmented it with a suggestion of a bow, although this to Sim was the rankest hypocrisy. Doctor Harewood, he noted, had trouble looking into his eyes. Sim eyed Harewood's pert neatness, wondering how he could deal in the sometimes unclean business of healing, and of dying, but Harewood rallied. He glanced up from under his grey wig as he raised his head.

'I am embarrassed, doctor, that so many of your patients have left you to return to me but, of course, I may with justice observe that they were once my patients.'

Sim drew up his eyebrows and sought out Harewood's rather satisfied eyes. 'What, however, may be the meaning of their leaving me, Sir? Might you offer me some explanation of it?'

'I, Sir?' said Harewood, who looked confused. Sim watched him closely and this, perhaps, explained the rush of colour in Harewood's face – but he was perfectly at a loss. 'Perhaps it is my many more years of experience?' Harewood tilted his head and cupped his cheeks. 'But I show you the symptom, Doctor Sim, not the disease.' He seemed pleased with this, and then indicated his waiting carriage that stood nearby on the road. 'I must be gone, Sir, pray excuse me. I have a number of patients awaiting me, one of whom is Mr Holyman, whose swollen joints are, I believe, not unknown to you?'

'Indeed,' replied Sim.

'Good morning, doctor,' said Harewood.

'Good morning.' Sim made way, but his manner suggested a desire to trip Harewood. Harewood, however, was much too sunny to be inconvenienced and, remarking on the pleasantness of the day, left Sim to watch him disappear along the dwindling road.

Chapter 8

A day or so after their arrival Bagshaw and Fanny sat waiting for breakfast. When they had eaten they were to go into town and purchase clothing for her. This pleased Fanny but displeased him, and he reiterated sternly that no luxuries would be purchased.

Despite this their errand excited her, as did the prospect of breakfast. For all her Sunday frock she sat at the table like a dog in the traps. Conversely, Bagshaw was indolent. He sat with his head resting heavily on his shoulders, so that his cheeks welled along his jaw.

'I also mean to give you instruction in charity,' he said. 'When we enter the city we will give away money.'

The look that she gave him was eloquent; she plainly thought that he was mad. The look that he gave her was also telling; in his opinion she showed a marked love of money. But he said nothing, although none the less made note.

'I should advise you to partake of a hearty breakfast,' Bagshaw said.

At this point he rang the bell for Bingley. The sudden thud of a money bag landing on the table startled Fanny, who had been busy contemplating food.

'You must know what it is to have, before you can ever know what it is to give. Have you a pocket, Fanny? Put it away. Later I shall require you to disperse it.'

33

Fanny reached out, her fingers grasped the bag and it was hers. Speedily she withdrew it. Bagshaw nodded. 'I may allow you to retain a few pennies as a gift, perhaps not, as a lesson in how hard and cruel life may be and how we must have fortitude against it.'

During their meal Bagshaw, who despised many of the niceties of table manners, mentioned the wolfish enthusiasm of Fanny for her food. This being done, straight it began again – but Bagshaw made note of referring to it some other time. For the moment Fanny was left in peace. Thus she was happy for the first time in her new life.

The prospect of happiness, material happiness that is to say, was uppermost in Fanny's mind as they went upon their errand. As they entered the town there was a penny candle burning within her. The sense of having a full belly also buoyed her mood. She was not used to such food. Her stomach approved of her new life; and the rest of her was yielding to it. She was already canny enough to show no pleasure in shopping but, in reality, she was thrilled. Before long, too, Bagshaw found a second-hand clothes shop and tailors, standing outside while Fanny was given up to be measured, only speaking to the shopkeeper, beyond the barest civility, to say what he was and was not prepared to purchase. The business was a dreary one for him.

'Would Sir like this? Would Sir like that? Would the young lady look well in this or that? This is the harder wearing, Sir, this the plainest, quite the blandest, this the least fashionable, this the . . .'

'Yes, yes, yes!' howled Bagshaw suddenly, hopping from one foot to another. The shopkeeper had not been slow to discern that Bagshaw would accede to every request, just to have done. Thus Fanny and the man formed an alliance, and several things were purchased that Bagshaw would not have ordinarily considered.

'Mr Bagshaw,' she said, innocently, 'which of these fabrics is most to your liking? This one, or this, or that one?'

'Take them all!'

Whereas to Bagshaw all this was a torture, to Fanny it was a delight. Before long many things had been purchased for her. Her new clothes must be made but she had second-hand clothes to wear in the meantime. Meekly she left the shop, and subjected herself to Bagshaw's appraisal. He was pleased that she was happy with second-hand things and so, happily enough, they moved off, with Fanny being careful to keep close to him among the people who thronged the town.

Lichfield was a focal point for many people who lived in the surrounding area and, of course, it had a population of its own. It was busy today and, to the unworldly eyes of Fanny, seemed like a metropolis. This was so much the case that at every step she found something that diverted her. It was difficult to watch where Bagshaw went. In this her lingering grief for the orphanage began to mix with a new and unsuspected excitement. She began to like Lichfield. Her place of birth, she thought, had been an industrial town. Oddly she remembered it by taste: there had been a tang of metal on the wind. She added to this the recollection of the noise of metal being worked. From Lichfield meadowland was in sight, and life was pleasing, not dominated by the thunderous commerce of iron. The air was clean, and this purity struck Fanny with delight; her communicating this to Bagshaw brought the most unsuspected pleasure to each. Bagshaw smiled and said something warm of simple things.

She trotted on in the wake of her master and was all eyes. So many people entered her world in passing: a fat, kindly housewife; a thin rake with mischief about him; children who eyed her; hawkers who caught her gaze in hope – as if she might intercede with Bagshaw! Fanny kept close through all these shoals, but her eyes, none the less, were fascinated by the people and intrigued by the buildings.

Among those who interested Fanny amid the normal run of persons were the clerics. These men shocked her by their poor dress and shoddy wigs. She thought too that one or two of them were drunk. Indeed, as she looked, there were other people about who had similar symptoms. She had seen a number of taverns, she recollected. Moreover, she noticed Bagshaw stiffen and thought that she detected displeasure in his bland, unexcited eyes. His defensiveness frightened her somewhat and with these drunken vicars, these packed crowds, she kept still closer to him.

Eventually Bagshaw slowed, and stopped within a few yards of a turning. Here, it seemed, he intended to distribute their largesse. This was the market-place, where a number of roads met. The place was eminently suitable, and he readied himself – encouraging Fanny to do the same.

It said much about Fanny's quickness that she saw reserve in Bagshaw as they prepared to distribute their coins; she realised how much he gave of himself. She respected this example, although Bagshaw was unaware that he had given it. She was inspired to recover from her person some coins that she had appropriated, and these were added to the common pot. This was a generous gesture, one of which Bagshaw approved, although Fanny still had one or two more tucked away.

Thus they began. Bagshaw began to run his eye over the people who passed him, as a farmer might buying sheep at market. The infirm, the old, mothers with children, those poorly dressed were all likely, without their expecting it, to find the big, chubby face at theirs, see the large, kind eyes and hear his sympathetic voice. 'Here you are. Go your way now, and I shall remember you should I see you again.' And so find a coin pushed into their hands, a hand at their back at the same time, obliging them, gently, not to abuse his charity.

In this fashion Bagshaw made way through his coins and began to enjoy himself, but there was a great traffic in people, and this scarcely allowed him to stop once having begun; he was also so fair that he hated to miss any who would otherwise have benefited. But at the first chance he stood back. He straightened, like a labourer rising from his work, and looked at Fanny. He was surprised at something: he found pleasure in sharing giving with the girl; her satisfaction seemed to multiply his. As before, they shared a moment of concord as he caught her eye and smiled, but he seemed blind to something, although, perhaps, he only pretended ignorance. Fanny was troubled, however, and the more so as they went on, because of the gathering of people near them. Perhaps this was in his mind when he smiled in catching her eye, and she felt something good about him and liked him for it; although the watchers did not go away.

It was perhaps the hope of some that Bagshaw would forget them and give a second time; or perhaps they hoped to play on the weakness, as they might have seen it, that had brought him there. Some, however, did not think of Bagshaw at all. Fanny was the more interesting to them, being but a girl, and they eyed her with the acuity that living on their wits had sharpened. She would be the easier to importune. Bagshaw, however, paid them no regard. Among these people were several tavern men, and they could see Bagshaw for what he was: none would try to cower or coerce him into giving more; moreover he was such a big man and strong looking. Bagshaw, though, when this was said, was a man on his own and had but one pair of eyes, so they waited for any opportunity that might come.

This atmosphere became such that it unsettled Fanny. She began to find less pleasure in what they did. All she wished for, in truth, was to go. Of a sudden, however, she was encouraged in seeing Miss Wagstaff and a gentleman. Fanny waved, a gay little wave, entirely unconstrained. There were still some yards between them, but they saw her, although the gentleman was not warm. Fanny would remember his expression later. Her spontaneity was to him, it seemed, too much like vulgarity. Miss Wagstaff, though, was as warm as he was cold. She smiled briefly but her eyes were knowing, and, so far as her manners would permit, she gave the girl a wave that was almost as warm as her own.

Mr Bagshaw briefly acknowledged Miss Wagstaff and her companion. He was too busy to say much, but it pleased him that Miss Wagstaff had come. Thus she might see this useful lesson being imparted. Indeed, he flattered himself that he had already left his stamp on Fanny. Frankly, how could she not profit from good example? Unfortunately, unknown to him, the example Fanny desired to emulate was that of Miss Wagstaff. She was quite the fashionable creature that Mr Bagshaw so despised, but she was lovely.

Fanny was wise enough to hide this admiration from Bagshaw, but such was the effect of Miss Wagstaff's attention that she became reinvigorated. Excitedly she took her money out and showed it to her friend. Bagshaw did not notice this, but it did not escape other notice. For a moment Fanny caught the eyes of Miss Wagstaff, but they were both soon distracted.

There was a movement – one of people jostling inwards – that unsettled Fanny. She sought reassurance from Bagshaw, who continued as before. He tried to hide from her that he, too, thought that they were too closely pressed. Thereafter events took a speedy turn. Just before she became frightened, just before she felt the weight of Bagshaw press into the crush, Fanny, as she remembered later, had been aggrieved. The man with Miss Wagstaff had clearly not the slightest indulgence to offer her. It seemed that he viewed her, and Mr Bagshaw, as creatures of an unwholesome sort.

It was at this point that Fanny had succumbed to the crush upon her. People were all round her; she could hardly keep her feet. The people seemed distorted: their greed, their lack of gratitude, their years were all magnified for her; and then she felt their hands on her. She screamed, and saw Bagshaw push into the crush – but she could not stand it. Up went the money in a showering of many pennies, and at once there was bedlam.

The next moments were hardly coherent for Fanny; they passed in a series of impressions. Some of the mob began to investigate her dress and person too, perhaps suspecting that she had more money hidden away, as indeed she had. This made her breathless and she screamed again. Bagshaw was fighting his way to her; and how formidable he was! She had a sudden wild hope in him, although she noticed, too, how he struggled among the bodies, like a bear she had once seen in a painting with dogs hanging from its every limb. He continued despite this to try and reach her.

But it was not Bagshaw who reached her first, it was Miss Wagstaff. Quite how she did this was not clear: she was not robust and wore a dress unsuited to a street brawl. Indeed, her hat had been knocked sideways when she reached Fanny. She was white too and there was a light in her eyes that Fanny knew to be fear, but Miss Wagstaff reached her, for all this, and having done so turned her back on them all, holding Fanny in a grip of steel, pressing her against the building that had been to the girl's rear.

The impression that Fanny had entertained of the man who was with Miss Wagstaff was augmented at this point. There passed a moment of the most surprising clarity. Just as Miss Wagstaff took her up Fanny caught sight of him. He stood on the margin, like a dog called to fetch a stick from water who does not wish to get his paws wet. She felt a sort of bitterness toward him, although, clever girl as she was, she saw, too, his impotence and shame.

'Ho,' she heard him call, trying to summon some sort of authority, some deference, which he seemed to think might be owed to him. 'Ho, mind that lady, mind that lady, I say!' But a moment later Miss Wagstaff had turned her to the wall.

It was at this point that Mr Bagshaw reached them, just after a seedy, bald, sweaty fellow had laid hands upon Miss Wagstaff, having probed Fanny and no doubt thinking that the woman might be more to his liking; indeed, he might have taken any liberty. Most certainly he would have ransacked her person, but with one straight blow Bagshaw felled him and the man fell backwards into the mob. Here he was supported until, the crowd's movement being such, he fell and landed amongst their feet in the gutter. This was no sooner done than Bagshaw, roaring 'Make way, Make way!', took up both Miss Wagstaff and Fanny and, by his own and their weight, and his sheer force, blundered and buffeted his way into the blessed open space of the street.

Their escape had been made; none followed them, as the crowd fought too much amongst itself. It would be difficult to exaggerate their relief in this moment. The joy of this was such that they quickly thought to move on. The last thing that they wanted was to be caught in the crowd once again.

When, finally, they were far from the mob and when they were sure that they were not pursued, they were able to stop, gather themselves and reflect; and Miss Wagstaff finally let Fanny go. Doctor Harewood was now all fuss and bother.

'Your help, Sir,' said Bagshaw, 'had been kind, had it been early.'

Poor Harewood winced. The remark was not kind and nor was it mannerly. It was not meant to be, but Doctor Harewood was not accustomed to being spoken to so and was affronted. What might he say, however? He was ashamed not to have been more active and mortified that this had been noticed, but such was Bagshaw's indifference that Harewood had no choice but to ignore it. Later Bagshaw regretted the remark, but for the moment he was angry, and only by degrees lost the wildness in his eyes. He was presently too inflamed for Harewood to do anything but remain silent, although Miss Wagstaff was of a different mettle.

'Mr Bagshaw, I wonder that you would expose Fanny to such a rabble. Surely you might have known that such a scene would occur? I wonder at you, Sir, I plainly own it.'

Bagshaw cast a dark look in her direction, but by now he was regaining his composure. For a moment he wondered whether he might ignore this riposte, but finally spoke. 'How is Fanny to learn charity and generosity except by giving? Besides this, Madam, I should have her know her good fortune and the hardship that there is in the world.'

Bagshaw straightened his own attire as a rather unsettled Miss Wagstaff, aided by the solicitous doctor, straightened her linen cap and hat; and, this being done, inspected some damage to her fine clothes. Fanny watched, all eyes, seeing that Mr Bagshaw was not yet finished.

'And to whom would you have Fanny give? The rich? What happened was unfortunate but I should have Fanny' – something of an abstracted look gained tenure of his face – 'courageous as a savage child or one of the young maidens of Sparta.' He turned to Fanny, not unkindly but without indulgence. 'You must endeavour, Madam, not to lose your composure on another such occasion.'

Fanny was not a little hurt by this and rather deflated. Miss Wagstaff saw this. 'Mr Bagshaw,' she said, 'the child is but ten and has only just been separated from her fellows. And more, your scheme can hardly have had opportunity to prosper in so short a time.'

'Oh indeed,' admitted Bagshaw, 'but I expect courage to rise with danger, Miss Wagstaff.'

While Bagshaw might well have continued, unfortunately it became clear that he had exhausted the patience of Miss Wagstaff. 'I must beg you to excuse me, Mr Bagshaw. I have had my fill of you for today. I bid you good afternoon, Sir, Fanny. Come, Doctor Harewood.' And with this she left them, stamping away down Breadmarket Street with the doctor in her wake, until within a minute she was gone from sight. Bagshaw stood a moment to stare after her. She had stung him with her sharp words although, unknown to him, she had noticed his courage in the fracas; and he, as he thought of it, was impressed by her, thinking her to be a Spartan herself, for all her fashionable dress.

He placed a hand on Fanny's shoulder and they returned home, all their lessons learnt for the day.

Chapter 9

Miss Wagstaff stood in her father's museum with Doctor Harewood. He was in good humour and shifted his weight from one leg to another.

'I was my mother's favourite child,' he said. 'My early promise singled me out. I was generally considered to be a child prodigy . . .'

Miss Wagstaff smiled.

'I may say,' he said, 'without complacency, that I have always been the bosom friend of acclaim. 'Twas so when I was a college man. When I received my degree, Ma'am, I was carried about the rival colleges shoulder high; shoulder high, Ma'am.'

'We are most fortunate to have you among us.'

'Indeed!' Doctor Harewood agreed. 'Thank you.' This remark had been ironic but it greatly encouraged him. 'When I came to this city, there had been no advancement in medicine since the time of Sir John Floyer.'

He narrowed his eyes and nodded. She, frowning, nodded at him.

'But, being singled out by Providence is an onerous thing. You have no idea, Madam, what it is to be born gifted.'

'Indeed!' Miss Wagstaff laughed. 'It must be a blessing, yet a burden, to be so much the better of everyone around you.' She smiled sweetly, inclined her head and was all innocence, although, of course, there was a barb to this.

Harewood stopped and this time suspected something. 'You tease me.'

'Yes.' Oh dear. She had not meant to give offence, but the doctor looked about him as if seeking the source of a stink. He turned to the window, leaving her mortified. Already, however, he had begun to think of something else – his dead wife. She would not have teased him, which had brought her to his mind.

'My wife would have loved this day,' he said, looking back. 'I believed that I should never be happy again when she died.' He smiled. 'But life renews itself.' Doctor Harewood stepped forward. 'You do right to tease me. I am ripe for it.' The lines puckered at the corners of his eyes and she raised her face to look at him; then he kicked a basket at his feet. Harewood glanced at it, and a thought seemed to occur to him. 'I hear that Sim is reduced to treating the common people of the town. Several persons of quality have given him up. I tell you, Madam,' he bobbed up and down, 'my prospects are excellent!'

'I believe' she said, 'that Doctor Sim has always provided his services to the poor of this town, whether or not they might pay him.'

'Aye,' replied Harewood, 'so that he may try his crack-brained treatments on them. Why, I have it that he makes all sorts of impositions upon them; people who have not the confidence to oppose him or the means to go elsewhere.'

'No, Sir. He would not undertake any treatment unless for the good of the person concerned.'

'Miss Wagstaff,' he said, 'you are so generous.' He brought her hand to his lips and his eyes, as he looked into hers, were kind, with a hint of self awareness. 'You are right, the fellow does some good. But I do as much. I am a trustee of the Turnpike Trust. I attend the pensioners of St John's Hospital and have substantial investments in the manufactories of this county.' He saw her eyes become unreceptive and added, 'In the thousands of miles that I travel each year, relieving suffering, I do good too, and this means more to me than fees.'

He was rather injured in saying this; he projected his nose at such an angle that she smiled. As ever, this was like the sun coming out. The admiration that he had for her was now very evident, and as ever it left her slightly ambivalent. This being so, even she liked being an object and sometimes felt grateful for it.

She also saw some way into him, and knew that he was not a bad man. Unlike Harewood, however, Miss Wagstaff had not prepared for his visit, and perhaps this was telling. Today she wore a white cap and, though her dress was attractive, it was much mended. However, as she knew, it showed the white of her arms in relief, and just enough of her shape to augment the appeal of her eyes and glossy hair. She smiled at him now and meant to find the cause of Doctor Sim's recent misfortune, if she might. Harewood, however, was distracted. He bent down to the box at his feet, so she bided her time.

'I know,' he said, 'that your cat has lately died, and could not forbear but to give you this kitty. I do hope that it meets with your approval.'

'Doctor Harewood, thank you!'

Harewood produced a kitten, which, with its plaintive meow and blue eyes, was soon nestling in her arms. Like a new father he stood and watched her.

'Your remark about Doctor Sim made me curious,' she said. 'That he has been reduced to treating common people. What may be the cause of this?'

'You seem very interested in that gentleman.'

'I wonder that you are not, if a doctor's standing may, so swiftly, be undermined without apparent cause.'

'There may be cause enough.'

'Pray Sir, what do you mean by that?'

Harewood had shifted slightly and she came round him that she might face him. His irritation that this subject had intruded upon them made him quite another man. He kept his head down, pressing his lips tight, but recovered himself. 'Why do you ask me, Miss Wagstaff?'

'Did you not allude to some knowledge of a cause?'

'I know what is commonly known. I wonder that you do not yourself know it. Perhaps you think me the originator of the exposé?'

'Of what do you speak?'

Harewood saw that she was in earnest. He rested his eyes on her a moment and then let out a long expiration of air, seeing that he must continue to talk of Sim whether he wished it or not. 'Have you not seen the *Gentleman's Magazine*, Miss Wagstaff? I know Mr Wagstaff sometimes obtains it. There is a poem in it that concerns Doctor Sim.'

Miss Wagstaff was interested by this, wondering after the nature of the poem and who might have written it. She saw, however, that any further enquiry might be fruitless and, more so, rude, since her guest so little shared her interest. She tried to prick him, though. 'I wonder', she said, 'who might have written such a piece? To be sure it was a cowardly thing to do.'

She watched him as she said this. He was exasperated, plainly enough, but nothing exactly condemned him, nor was he acquitted. If the doctor knew, or had done it, he would not say. She took her eyes from him, finally, but his visit thereafter, saving odd interludes, became a succession of half-developed snatches of conversation, and she was relieved when he left.

She stood at the door and watched him as he departed, and once she was sure that he had gone she sent a servant to obtain the magazine. Within the space of twenty minutes she had it. The poem shocked and disgusted her. It attacked Sim's religious views and, considering the assurance that he had given her, seemed one of misinformation and spite. It also had the stamp on it of cowardice; and so she sat down to write.

Although Sim's work had been much reduced he was out that afternoon when the letter arrived. It lay in his hall some while, but at last he read it as he sat in the firelight. He was tired. He had spent some hours that afternoon with a woman who had been drinking heavily to relieve a painful condition. She had died. Sim blamed himself that he had been slow to notice her alcoholism, and wished that it might have been different.

The mood of the room in which the woman had died clung to him and he was in need of cheer; consequently he was thankful for Miss Wagstaff's letter. The letter now lay on the table beside him, next a copy of the *Gentleman's Magazine* and part of this he recited aloud, in a soft voice.

At Lichfield Sim casts his magic spells,
Over patients, bones, cats and cockle shells . . .

His voice trailed away and became a mutter, but the end of the poem caught his eye and he spoke it:

And trawling round the clerics for his fee,

Is seldomly himself upon his knee:
Denying his Creator, saying all,
Originated in the briny squall.

He was an inventor, the poem said, not to be trusted; a mechanic, a zany, a quack. He repeated the word 'quack' to himself two or three times and then, at length, got up. He took the letter from the table, walked stiffly to one of the two candles on the mantelpiece and re-read it.

My Dear Doctor Sim,
I have written, Sir, to warn you of some mischief against your reputation. It seems that a poem has appeared in the 'Gentleman's Magazine' which I believe may injure you.
I cannot say who may have penned this work, although I have a suspicion of it, but I do entreat you to obtain a copy so that the attack may be countered.
In closing, Sir, I beg you to remove the motto from your carriage doors which can only serve to hurt you.
When my father finds the magazine I cannot tell how he may react to it but I shall do my best to placate him, should this be necessary.
I remain your friend,
Jenny Wagstaff

Sim read this and idled over it, leaning an elbow upon the mantelpiece. He stood so long that he grew hot and smelt the fabric of his coat before he returned to his chair. He was, by turns, angry and moved: angry that someone had slandered him, yet moved that Miss Wagstaff should warn him of it. She had a warm heart, he decided.

At length he got up and glanced at the clock. It was 11.30 at night but he considered calling upon Harewood. However, if Harewood admitted that he had written the poem Sim felt something unseemly might happen, and such was his annoyance, and his temper, that he could not say how this might end. Beside this, he did not believe that Harewood would admit it. No, there must be another way to settle their account, but he had no doubt that Harewood had penned the verse, none at all.

Before he climbed the stairs to bed Sim briefly thought

45

about Mr Wagstaff. He hoped that there would be no repercussions in that quarter. He was also concerned whether the damage he had suffered might grow worse, and this worried him. Again his annoyance flared and he marched across the room, shutting the door loudly, and went to bed, leaving the room to the shadows and the subsiding fire.

Chapter 10

A day or so after the fracas in the city Bagshaw sat and read with Fanny. He wanted to improve her reading, and used cards on which words had been broken into syllables. He noted how quick she was to learn.

Fanny was a rewarding pupil and had gained much knowledge since she had left the orphanage. She wanted to please, and her eyes, as she watched him, were keen. She had conceived what would become a passion for learning, and had he tired of his experiment and sent her back it would have been hugely cruel. Fanny had begun to sense the potential of life. Moreover, she was spruce in her new clothes, and this excited her, too. She was pretty and knew it: long haired, with brown eyebrows and a hint of womanhood about her, which Bagshaw idly noticed in directing the lesson; although her eyes were still those of a child.

'Fanny.'

The girl was pleased that he called her, although her mind had strayed to Miss Wagstaff and her lovely clothes. However, she turned with all her attention in his direction.

'What is a blockhead?'

After a moment's thought the girl brightened. 'A numbskull.'

'Yes. And how should we treat them?'

She was not so quick in answering this and glanced at the

listening face of Bagshaw, who said nothing. 'You doh lend 'em money.'

'Perhaps.' Bagshaw was dissatisfied.

'You treat 'em with the contempt they deserve.' Fanny suggested this, remembering it from somewhere and sure that it was the right thing to say, but Bagshaw shook his head.

'A man may be foolish but still be a good man. He may perhaps be misguided, even stupid in his actions, but he may still be good. What is in the heart is the real estimation of a man. Remember that, Fanny.'

Bagshaw nodded, and began to consider another bastion to assault, but then the doorbell rang. Thereafter they waited the slow progress of the servant. Bagshaw got to his feet, animated by the long wait.

The thought that their visitor came unannounced made Bagshaw wonder who it was; then Bingley entered and said that Mr Wagstaff and Harewood had come. Bagshaw was unprepared, but they had come and so it was. It was a rule with him to meet the unexpected as though expected. In this he hoped always to behave as he ought, but none the less he was a little uneasy. Fanny saw his brows sink over his eyes; and, unknowing, his mouth pugged up. But when the guests entered Bagshaw had regained his seat, and was attempting to look more indolent and unmoved than before. Fanny was excited: company had that effect upon her.

It took an effort of some will, it seemed, for Bagshaw to get to his feet, but he was civil, after his fashion. The men were very polite, but once cordialities were over there was a moment of uncertainty between them. Bagshaw waited, saying nothing.

'So,' said Mr Wagstaff, at last. 'This is the young lady of whom we have heard. Goodness, Doctor Harewood, what a fine young girl. May I look at the child, Mr Bagshaw? I must squint, I'm afraid; my eyes are not what they were.'

Their request to study Fanny was referred by Bagshaw to the girl. She had not the confidence to refuse but she resisted, inspecting them as they did her. Indeed Mr Wagstaff was a curious animal. She considered the matter. He had a face like a bulldog pup. Doctor Harewood was more presentable, but he had offended Fanny a day or so before. Taller, younger and not unhandsome, with grey eyes and a long nose, he was dressed in a

48

bushy wig and a fine coat of a plum colour. Everything about him was just as it ought to be. He, too, peered at her. Fanny had last seen this expression when Mr Bates had bought a pig. She blushed, but some pride in her made her glare back.

'Are you *quite* well, my dear?'

The solicitous tone, so unlike his attitude of before the riot, disgusted Fanny. 'I 'ave a lot to eat,' she said, 'An' I've got these new things.'

'Are you *quite* well?' asked Mr Wagstaff. The old man narrowed his eyes. She unconsciously copied him, so that they nodded at each other. He became secretive and so did she. The old man's head bobbed and so did hers. When he stuck his jaw out and raised his eyebrows, though, she did not copy him. She was also confused by this emphasis on 'quite'. She glanced at Bagshaw, but he stood like a bull stake and would not help. There had been civility enough, she thought, but Bagshaw seemed nettled.

'Quite well,' Fanny said. Harewood and Wagstaff looked at each other. Mr Wagstaff resumed his consideration of her and Bagshaw folded his arms across his chest. All this added to the expectation of something. She did not know, as they did, that he was waiting for any accusation of impropriety.

'Indeed,' said Harewood, reddening but chancing Bagshaw's eyes. 'We meant no offence in coming here. Upon my honour, Sir, we were at leisure and decided to call, not having had opportunity to properly make your acquaintance before now.'

Bagshaw puffed out his cheeks. He said nothing audible but disbelief was plain in him.

'Tosh!' said Mr Wagstaff. Poor Harewood, who had looked for corroboration, winced in the sure knowledge of being disappointed. 'Mr Bagshaw knows our business very well. We came, Sir, to discover what sort of man you were.' Wagstaff was entirely unapologetic. As Bagshaw grew stiff and looked even larger Wagstaff scuttled forward. 'Why, Sir, it is not natural. You have here a young girl about you, not your daughter and not yet eleven, but you live together so and mean to train her as a wife! It will not do, Sir, it will not do.'

'Out with it!' might have been the motto of the old man. He had said what he had a mind to, and it was for Bagshaw to make of it what he might. To this end he pottered up and down with his nose in the air: 'Pooh!' he said at his farthest extent, hand upon his hip. 'Pooh!' he repeated, once he returned to them. Bagshaw, for his part, had a delicate sense of honour. Without the least embarrassment he ran his eyes over the old man. As he considered, however, he found some empathy with his guests. In truth, Wagstaff's scepticism was not unreasonable. Consequently he did not resent it. There came two, three and more tick-tocks from the clock in the corner, and then Bagshaw reacted. He put his hands on his hips and laughed.

'Upon my word, Sir, you are rude, but you are at least direct. There is some merit in that. Allow me, then, to present testimonials of my moral character.'

Bagshaw went immediately to a drawer and began flinging things from it, but Mr Wagstaff turned to the doctor. The piggy eyes opened wide. 'Rude, eh?' – huff, huff, puff, puff – 'Eh? The fellow says that I'm rude, Harewood!'

'Perhaps we have troubled Mr Bagshaw long enough?' said Harewood.

'Pooh!' grunted Wagstaff.

The old man did not enjoy being called rude, but Harewood sighed. He wished that they had not come. Mr Wagstaff tossed his head about and would have made more of his humiliation, but the doctor at last came forward and took the testimonials.

'Forgive us, Sir. We do not know you.'

As the men settled over the papers – letters from a bishop, from a peer of the realm, from a judge of the High Court and sundry gentlemen – Bagshaw explained his business. Fanny was to be brought up to be rational. She would be made perfect by good example. She would learn to recognise folly and vice and be disgusted by them, whilst prizing truth and goodness. She was to love virtue, see the merit of industry, be capable of relying upon herself, be Christian – without being bound to any denomination – and, in sum, be natural, without her native goodness being corrupted by aught that was false or base.

'And, may I say,' said Bagshaw, 'that I am well satisfied with her progress.'

Fanny, following this discussion with her eyebrows bent like

50

viaduct arches, now blinked and smiled, a very grateful, natural smile.

'Up to now,' said Bagshaw.

The doctor had gained some confidence by the manner in which Bagshaw had responded to Mr Wagstaff, and now raised his voice; there was a suggestion of condescension about him. He was still annoyed by Bagshaw's remark to him after the fracas in the city, and would have been glad to repay him in kind.

'Come, Sir, I have heard of such children, raised and educated according to supposed "natural" principles, but do they not always end in running wild?'

'Fanny will not run wild,' said Bagshaw, his meaty chops bunching around his straight-line mouth.

'Mr Bagshaw,' added Mr Wagstaff. He had now graciously put aside his annoyance. The old man brought his hands together and smiled: a fond, indulgent, weary, worldly-wise smile, such as narrowed Bagshaw's eyes in expectation of what might follow. 'You are very young, hardly past your majority. Know you your business, my dear young Sir?'

'I know no business of yours, Sir, in talking to me so.'

This remark upset once again the sensibility of Mr Wagstaff. The old man set off on one of his tottering walks. A tremor ran through him, he gave forth a succession of grunts and a hand found its way back onto his hip. While he paraded, Bagshaw adopted a posture of perfect indifference but poor Harewood was at a loss. He briefly considered remarking upon the weather. Instead he let out a long expiration, wishing only to go, but was saved. For the first time Fanny became uncomfortable; and her taking Bagshaw's hand embarrassed their visitors.

The men were gentlemen and neither Harewood nor Wagstaff wished to upset the child.

'Believe me,' said Harewood, 'I see you for an upstanding man, but as you have this week caused a riot in this town, are we not to wonder at your course of action?'

'I?' Bagshaw coloured. 'I brought aid. I saw no other being given.' He grew warm as he thought of this charge. Giving them a moment for response, he then continued. 'It may be of interest' Bagshaw said, his legs wide in a splendid pose, 'that divers drunken parsons were, on that day, exhibiting in the streets of

51

this city. I should like to talk of that.'

'Hold, Sir,' said Wagstaff. 'Hold.' He held up a hand. 'Do not abuse our clergy, Sir, drunk or not.'

'You should be aware, Sir,' interjected Harewood, becoming warm, 'that the circumstances attending the riot are being investigated.'

'What is that to me?' said Bagshaw. 'Let Lucifer investigate it.'

'Steady, Sir!' Mr Wagstaff was appalled. 'This is heady talk.' He was rather heady, too, but he was not without kindness and smiled at the girl. Although missing some teeth, with brows like a worn-out brush, he tried to be agreeable – as he saw that the child was not pleased by their conversation.

'You must understand,' said Harewood, 'the position that we hold in this city. We are pillars, Sir, pillars of this community.'

'In short,' said Wagstaff, 'we are a decent set of people.'

'Good,' replied Bagshaw, 'for so are we.'

When this was said he had nothing more to say. For this reason he said nothing, and the company fell into silence. For a minute they did no more than look at one another. Thus they continued in awkwardness until, at last, Bagshaw decided that he wanted them gone. 'Well,' he said, 'if you would excuse us, gentlemen, I must proceed with Fanny's education.'

The gentlemen did not seem minded to excuse them, but whether they did or not the bell was rung for Bingley. Tolerably correctly, none the less, the gentlemen were escorted from the room, and at last they were gone.

'We are becoming known,' Bagshaw said when the door was shut; but thereafter he regained his chair and prepared to continue, quite as if nothing had occurred. Fanny now had a face longer than a canal barge. 'Now, Fanny,' he said, 'remember your lesson.'

Fanny thought, and a light kindled behind her eyes in thinking. She laughed – a little musical tinkle – the first time that she had laughed since her adoption; and Bagshaw laughed with her.

'I am sure that they meant well,' he said. He dropped heavily onto his chair. 'But I doubt that we shall be dining with them.'

Thereafter they went on as before, and the day proceeded very happily into evening.

Chapter 11

Sim, whose work remained slack, had an hour or so of leisure, and he and Miss Wagstaff were walking together. In truth the doctor had sought her out, although he pretended an accident. Sim was dispirited and wished for company, troubled as he was by the poem, and hoped to talk himself into a better mood.

The land where they walked was on the southern side of the cathedral. Today it was a space of flowers, water-loving plants and sunlight on water, but in the Civil War it had been a battleground. Where they walked had been a no-man's land, within musket shot of the town and Close.

Where the shot had flown the Close gardens ran down to the pool. There were trees along the water, and through these they could see the red brick Close. The houses, in their quiet repose, were pleasing but one hardly looked at them, such was the view of the cathedral that loomed over them. It was a view that never failed to impress, and both Sim and Miss Wagstaff stared for some minutes at it.

From the pool they walked to the east and within a short time passed along a picket fence, behind which lay another pool. This was Stowe Pool, which extended almost as far as St Chad's Church, about four hundred yards away. The church was a beacon of sorts, and without thought they began to saunter toward it.

It was now that time of year which Sim had longed for in the winter, and in token of this he delighted in some bright yellow flowers – but would not pick them. Instead he got down, stretching one booted leg behind him and bending the other at the knee, contriving to get his nose inside them. Miss Wagstaff narrowed her eyes against the light and watched him, smiling. This was not what she expected of a gentleman, but it seemed to suit him. The flowers were nearly spent and he got up, exaggerating the effort. He rearranged his full wig, and she stepped forward to brush some greenery from his coat. It was something that gave them both pleasure. He liked to have her fuss round him and she was surprised to enjoy it herself.

The coat was a long one, with many buttons down its front in two rows, a vivid blue and of a summer weight. Sim wore this with a waistcoat and white shirt, while Miss Wagstaff was attired as if to ride. Her riding clothes were inspired by male dress, a bold fashion for a provincial city. Sim thought them charming. At her neck she had a white cravat and her hair was dressed and gathered. This was immaculate, but Sim lamented that powder had denuded its lustre of rich black-brown. Finally she had a hat, which was pinned in place at something of a jaunty angle.

'You, Madam, are a very model,' said Sim. Miss Wagstaff inclined her head and smiled, enquiring. Sim indicated some buildings on the other side of the lake. 'The world might have it, Miss Wagstaff, that you have a head for fashion and nothing else, but such an assumption would be quite wrong.'

'Indeed, Doctor Sim, for I know several things, a dozen at least!'

Sim had earlier talked of the buildings in connection with the production of leather. The water supply that was so ready had, in part, encouraged tanners to work hereabouts, and there was a parchment maker's too, not far from them. He had made the error of assuming that she knew nothing of it, but she did. It was an error that he often made. He sometimes forgot that others, too, might have knowledge or understanding.

'So great a man as you are, Doctor Sim, there is still a small share of knowledge to be found among the rest of us.'

Sim looked a little embarrassed for a moment; he was conscious of some of his faults and vain enough to hate that they should be pointed out to him, but she smiled. There was a light of mischief in her eyes that he had learned to recognise and come to enjoy. She glanced at him now, and her black brows framed the white light of this. She put her chin down and her cheeks rounded a moment, and Sim at once launched into another project that he wanted to introduce.

'Indeed, Madam, I know you for a good, sombre, decent country maid and a veritable bluestocking. Therefore be pleased to consider this: I should like to devise a plan of female education and wish for your help. I am wholly opposed to the idea that women should cultivate domestic virtues and sensibility at the expense of strength, both of body and of mind.'

Miss Wagstaff had stopped, rather surprised, and, more than this, flattered. None the less, she meant to test him.

'Perhaps you might more usefully apply to Mr Bagshaw?' she said.

'No,' replied Sim. 'I have asked you.'

She was pleased at this. She had not really wanted Sim to approach Bagshaw and set her head a moment on one side, an unconscious gesture, and set to thinking. 'I should wish that strong moral tenets be imparted based on religious principles.' She caught Sim's eyes for a moment in a decided manner.

Sim began to move on. 'The principles are good ones,' he agreed.

'And I think exercise to be essential,' she said, as she scampered lightly in the doctor's wake. The interest of their conversation had quickened his thoughts and walking.

'Indeed,' said Sim. 'And modern languages.'

'And economy and science.'

'Yes,' said Sim. 'Yes!'

He stopped and took in a great draught of fresh air. As he did so he turned to her as she came up and smiled. He was immensely pleased. He put his hands on his hips and, without reserve, peered under the brim of her hat, wanting to share his enthusiasm. For her part, she gazed at him. She was drawn to the great good naturedness of him, and his red ploughboy cheeks, and she smiled at his talkativeness, watching the working of his lips with his good teeth behind them as he chatted on. Suddenly he stopped and took her arm, pointing.

'Before long,' Sim said, 'swallows will be over this water and the fields, turning round, at speed, within the width of a lane. It makes one sad, almost, for the people who must lose them, but they come to us!'

Miss Wagstaff understood him well, and together they ran their eyes over the pool – but were disappointed to find no swallows. 'I see them in my mind's eye,' she replied. So it was that they turned aside, looking for something else to please them. Each expected to be pleased; the only question was what it would be that they settled on. Naturally, it seemed, they looked to the cathedral, each enjoying the same thing but without either having to say what it was. The cathedral seemed like a castle from a fairy tale, the spires like the towers of a childhood story. Sim began to talk again, ludicrously it might have seemed, about his talking machine, but, inspired as he was, it was natural that his mind should turn to science. She understood this. There were two or three gentlemen of science corresponding with him on the subject. He had been drawn to their notice by the scurrilous poem about him. 'You see,' he said, 'everything turns out for the best.' Sim hoped to invite them to see the machine as soon as it was made.

Miss Wagstaff professed herself to be tired and she lent upon his arm as they made their way back toward the Close, still speaking of the talking machine, the sunlight warm on the water; and Sim, for all his anxiety about the poem, was almost happy.

Chapter 12

One fine morning Bagshaw looked towards the pool. Over the water he could see the cathedral: with its spires and high walls it seemed like a fairy castle or Camelot, a fancy that often occurred to him. The sun was warm and the grass beneath the window tipped in gold.

'Come, Fanny,' he said. 'Come.'

The girl looked up, surprised. Bagshaw was half across the room.

'Come, child!'

Such was the urgency of Bagshaw's appeal that she instantly left her task. A moment later the two of them were bounding down the stairs and bursting out into the garden, abreast like a wedding day couple. Bagshaw took her hand and led her out to the centre, the very widest point. There he bent, grinning, to the girl.

Once upon a time this energy, this enthusiasm, of Bagshaw's would have frightened Fanny, but she was in no way frightened now. She was, however, confused, and turned two willing but uncomprehending eyes on Bagshaw.

'Do you not feel the promise of the morning?' he asked. 'Do you not feel the tide of your young life rising inside you?'

Fanny frowned, having no idea what Bagshaw was talking of and hating to be confused. Her pretty face, all unlined, her fine eyes beneath her dark brows, grew thoughtful and then

57

nonplussed, and then somewhat frustrated. Bagshaw, meanwhile, grew ever more fidgety.

'Do you not feel your youth, Fanny? Do you not wish to run?' And saying this, Bagshaw in his coat, his waistcoat and boots began running round the garden, flicking up his heels, making capers and frisks, jumping and bounding. 'Come, Fanny, run, run! Feel the vitality of your young life, feel the strength of your limbs while you may do so, run!'

Unnoticed by Bagshaw – but perhaps he did notice it – Fanny enjoyed a laugh at him, but she began running, not without embarrassment at first. As she grew in confidence she was soon sprinting, leaping, cutting a dash and gambolling, and thus were they engaged when a carriage drew up in front of the house. Bagshaw saw it but did not care, and only when he was called by name, close, did he attend at all – and thus met the astounded, laughing eyes of Miss Wagstaff, her father and Sim.

While this amusement was generally vested among them, it varied in degree. Sim retained his good humour, like sleep, in his eyes and Miss Wagstaff showed similar symptoms, but Mr Wagstaff looked at Bagshaw with his mouth agape. Any laughter of his had a decidedly nervous character. Seeing them, Bagshaw finally stopped and, ruddy and breathing heavily, made a civil recognition of them all.

It was not his inclination to apologise for himself, and so he said nothing to explain what he had been doing. Mr Wagstaff attributed this to some mental deficiency, but Jenny respected it and smiled for, not at, him.

'Madam,' said Bagshaw, as the sun lit her eyes that moment, 'what felicity it affords me to feel the vigour of your young life. Today I see the green in you.'

Mr Wagstaff turned to Sim. 'The fellow talks of agriculture, Sim!' This remark was not as private as it might have been; in fact it was not private at all. Sim thought that it might be opportune to talk of something else.

'Mr Bagshaw,' he said, brightly, 'you are cordially invited to join our party at the loyal race day on Wednesday next.'

'Can I come?' This question emanated from Fanny, who said it in a voice that resembled a clap of thunder. This was not polite, especially for a child.

'Madam.' Bagshaw bent down to her, his large eyes seeking

hers. 'Convention dictates that you should not bawl out in the conversation of your elders. Since you must be able in life to adapt to the conditions about you, it is better that you learn not to repeat your offence.'

Fanny nodded to the big, stern eyes.

'However, since I wish you to be happy I now give you leave to express your happiness, since you are fortunate enough to feel any: therefore Hurrah! Hurrah!' He gave Fanny's arm a little prompting. 'Hurrah!'

'Hurrah,' shouted Fanny. 'Hurrah to the races!'

So it was that the matter was settled. In the hiatus that followed, the company was a little at a loss, and the idea of walking naturally suggested itself. This was very well. Less agreeable was the question of who should partner whom. Bagshaw pretended indifference, but would not have selected Mr Wagstaff – and Mr Wagstaff would not have chosen him. But so it was decided. Bagshaw walked with Mr Wagstaff, Sim with Miss Wagstaff and Fanny ran on ahead.

It was, of course, just as Mr Wagstaff and Bagshaw had feared. He and Mr Wagstaff made a sombre couple. Bagshaw, without conversation, said nothing but watched the sauntering walk of Sim, who inclined toward Jenny, probably with some nonsense. For want of something else Bagshaw listened to the rustle of her dress and watched her. Miss Wagstaff had all the glory of a peacock. He frowned at all the puffed-out bulk of her dress; he noted her built-up hair; he eyed her big hat, which was trimmed with ribbons. Oh, she was a fashionable creature, and yet he could not help but watch her.

Her father was troubled to have no conversation. Mr Wagstaff had been brought up to believe that a gentleman should be able to converse at will. He had nothing, however, to say, and Bagshaw, for his part, offered nought; but Wagstaff racked his brains for fodder.

'I remember, Sir, when I was of your age. I, too, had all manner of crack-brained schemes.' He offered this in perfect innocence, and was therefore confused by a sort of look that Bagshaw gave him: the rather dreamy eyes grew quite wide in passing. 'Oh,' said Wagstaff, realising his mistake, 'Don't mind me, Sir.'

The two walked on in silence, and Wagstaff grew anxious to

mend his unfortunate remark. As they walked he looked up, like a naughty boy, into Bagshaw's face, as his companion merely looked ahead. 'Indeed, Sir,' he lowered his voice and glanced a moment at his daughter, 'I've had some scrapes.' The small, piggy eyes became conspiratorial. 'To tell the truth, Sir, I've had many a tussle in the hay.'

Bagshaw seemed to have ingested a fly or something such.

'I shouldn't mind one now, Sir, if I could get it. Eh, Sir, eh!' Bagshaw scowled, and Wagstaff's reedy laugh sounded.

'Come!' said Mr Wagstaff. He adopted his shifty manner once again. 'I speak to you as a man. Had you not better find a wife and marry now? A fine strapping fellow like you? What of your animal spirits, Sir, eh?'

'Mr Wagstaff,' said Bagshaw, flatly. He stooped and turned his head round, his cheeks heavy and his eyes seeking out the old man. 'I must ask you to spare me any more such questions.'

'Ah,' said Mr Wagstaff. 'No more. Sorry. Bother.'

Thereafter the two men walked on in silence, a silence made deeper by the stubborn nature of them both, neither offering any diversion or chance of other conversation. Bagshaw had his cheeks bunched up and brows down; Wagstaff had his chops hanging but his nose up, wearing a baffled and somewhat cross expression; but they kept pace with each other for form's sake. Each one, for want of something, watched the sportive Fanny running about ahead. The occasional laughter from before them was now thoroughly irritating.

Sim was in full train. He had turned the conversation to carriages, and related an accident that had occurred. 'So, Miss Wagstaff, the fellow was driving his new friend home and suddenly asked if he had ever had a carriage accident. Pardon my language, Ma'am,' said Sim, catching her eye. "No," said the friend, "thank God." "Well," said the other, "What a dullard you have been all these years" – and promptly drove the carriage into a rock, throwing them both out into the gutter!'

Sim laughed, showing his good teeth, and the colour shone like apples in his cheeks. Miss Wagstaff also laughed, although in part at the doctor himself.

'Forgive me, Madam,' said Sim, 'I digress. I was talking of music. I wish that you might take me in hand and instruct me. I am most sadly deficient in this area, a circumstance I ascribe to a

60

tutor I had when young who used to call at our home to teach me music. However, the fellow rode to us and, if the hunt were in full cry, would be off. Goodness me, he had but a cob, which was much too small for him, all legs as he was, but off he would go, leaving me deprived of my lesson.'

Miss Wagstaff thought it unlikely that the doctor was in reality deficient in anything; moreover, she suspected that he meant to flatter her. She did not mind a little flattery, here and there, so she inclined her head and smiled, seeking his eyes, amused by him. The doctor adopted a very innocent face, although he knew and she knew that he was not really in need of tuition; but he pretended it, and that was their game.

Sim, though, quickly changed tack again, and was soon talking to her of engineering and his ideas of carriage design. Now she was flattered. The doctor clearly believed her able to understand the most complicated principles as, indeed, she might, and they had a very animated conversation.

Thus did their walk extend into the far rear of the garden, where fruit trees stood in rows bending their branches to the ground. The path went between the trees and the pairs in tandem strolled into the bower, the path being less a path than a track, also much overgrown. It soon became time for a change of partners, the garden boundary making a turn-about necessary, and so, after a moment or two of conversation, they began to return toward the front of the house, this time Sim walking with Mr Wagstaff and Bagshaw attending the daughter. For a moment he was also joined by Fanny. She was tired of running and tucked in behind him, but Sim called her back, and the doctor rested a hand on her shoulder as he strolled along talking pleasantly with the old man.

Thus Bagshaw was left in a silence all his own, and in the company of the charming Miss Wagstaff. She, as she had not been with Sim, was quiet. This did not embarrass Bagshaw, however, who took it for deference in his companion.

'Miss Wagstaff, I have lately made several additions to my library, which I should be pleased to send you if you wish it. I suggest Mr Rousseau, whom I think most instructive. Do not hesitate, Madam, should you require me to formulate a reading list for you.' Bagshaw smiled, his big cheeks becoming flushed, the fine eyes obliging, but Miss Wagstaff looked to the backs of their companions. She remained quiet and kept her face down, as if to watch the movement of each foot in turn, though her expression was thoughtful. Bagshaw began to recommend another project of self improvement. Suddenly she turned, fixed him firmly in the eyes (which pleased him in its boldness) and told him that she did not require his help. Bagshaw at once caught her meaning.

'Pardon me, Madam.'

She was placated, and Bagshaw's apologetic eyes were met by hers. Peeping under her hat brim, she allowed him to see that the matter was forgotten.

Thus they continued in the wake of the laughter and loud conversation that attended those in front, but Miss Wagstaff did not seem to miss this frivolity. Bagshaw appreciated that she might be serious-minded. He decided to reward this inclination.

'Tell me, Madam, is a man's judgment always superior to that of a woman's? Is this not a natural law? While women may have advantages in some respects, is a man not always supreme in reason?'

Miss Wagstaff reached out to divert a hanging twig. She remarked on the loveliness of the garden, and some snatch of the water close to the house, and of the city on the far side of it, and she commented on the far spires and held up a white hand to her hat brim. Bagshaw joined her in looking, and then they continued on their way. But still he wished to pursue the topic of their former conversation. He bent to her in mock sombreness.

'Miss Wagstaff, you will allow . . .'

'Mr Bagshaw,' she interrupted, and he was crushed. Her eyes were shadowed by her hat, but he saw enough of them for her meaning to be clear. 'I am not going to go on with this conversation, since you are determined to vex me.'

Bagshaw looked at her, rather askance. He had no meant to vex but to instruct. For a moment he was quite shocked. As he thought of it, though, he wished that he might be more obliging and less vexing. Since they were almost at the carriage, which had been brought to the near corner of the yard, he would imminently have to quit her company, and there was much more to be said.

She smiled in a very knowing and conciliatory way, a little embarrassed, perhaps, that Mr Bagshaw now seemed to have nothing to say, and neither had she.

Mr Wagstaff and Sim waited at the carriage. Miss Wagstaff was handed inside, and was followed by the men. After assurances that they would all meet again on Wednesday, the visitors took themselves away, and Fanny and a rather perplexed Bagshaw watched them go.

Chapter 13

The races were to be held at Whittington Heath, which was just outside the city. On the appointed day the road to Whittington was busy; most of the people of Lichfield seemed to be abroad.

The coach in which Sim's party travelled was designed to be commodious, but in spite of this it was crowded as it lumbered off the lane. With Sim were the Wagstaffs, Bagshaw, Fanny and Doctor Harewood, who was a late addition to the party. Harewood, in truth, had not been universally welcome. As they rattled along one or two of the group were ill at ease. Harewood said little to Sim, and frankly found Bagshaw trying, while Bagshaw did not speak at all. Miss Wagstaff felt somehow responsible for the happiness of them all, and shared her conversation among them.

For want of topics she initiated some discussion about the carriage, which was one of Sim's own design. One or two of the company made observations about it as they alighted, to which Sim, listening keenly, responded; and Harewood too, as he got out, studied it with great care.

'There, Sir, on the doors, has something not been painted out?' Harewood inclined to Sim with a thin smile.

Sim frowned. 'Yes, Sir.' It was a brief answer and once it was made he busied himself.

'I believe that I caught a glimpse of it one day, but did not understand it.'

'It was Latin,' said Sim.

Harewood smiled. Miss Wagstaff tried to distract everyone. She and Sim began to fuss about something.

'Oh, I understand Latin, Doctor.'

Miss Wagstaff glanced at Sim and noticed that, briefly, he touched his forehead with the tips of the fingers of one hand.

'It was the sentiment that confused me,' said Harewood, 'Everything from the sea.' What may be the meaning of that?'

Sim said nothing. He stood to his full height and looked at Harewood, perused him, one might have said. He clearly thought, but said nothing. The company stood round. The moment drew out.

Harewood looked at Sim with a smile like that of the showmen who played to the crowds in the striped booths about them; it was a look that might have invited them to throw money into his hat.

'The seas are so fecund,' said Sim.

'Oh. Indeed,' replied Harewood.

'Do these things ever mean anything?' said Mr Wagstaff with sudden impatience. 'Look at letter writing: "I shall wait upon you; I remain your humble servant," or "I am at your service." I am at your service! Try asking the fellow to fetch you a bushel of potatoes, eh, eh?'

This was very probably true but not altogether germane to the point at issue. Glances passed among the company. The remark was not strictly relevant but it would do, and it concluded this particular conversation. The old fellow waited for an answer but none came, and he moved off, quite expecting the others in the party to follow. The doctors broke their contact with each other, and Harewood tripped off after Mr Wagstaff. For a moment, though, Sim and Miss Wagstaff exchanged a look. She was embarrassed, frankly, and annoyed, too, with Harewood; but she also wondered about Sim's provocative motto. As she began to probe its meaning, she pondered about the nature of his religious convictions and how far the poet had traduced him.

'Miss Wagstaff,' said Sim, but she turned and left, and Sim had to broaden his stride to catch up with her.

'I know that the fossils are more than curiosities to you, Doctor,' she snapped, as they walked in the wake of her father and Doctor Harewood. The doctor sighed and, looking once to the back of Harewood, frankly wished him ill.

'You know you might undo me?' he asked.

Miss Wagstaff raised her head, and Sim felt he coloured. It was painful to him that she was guarded when there had been, he believed, the makings of some regard between them. In looking at him, her eyes were suspicious.

'I am not so fortunate', he said, speaking directly into her eyes, 'to share the faith that I know sustains you.'

She halted a moment in her walk. 'You told me that you did believe. Have you lied to me, Sir?'

'I am led, Miss Wagstaff,' he was sombre and stung by her manner, 'to believe in a different sort of Genesis. I maintain that we, everything we see about us, has arisen from a single filament and that life, generation upon generation, over thousands and thousands of years, age upon age, has diversified as branches do from the trunk of a tree.'

Miss Wagstaff was astonished. She had heard something of this before, but to be confronted with it! And she recalled how the devil may adopt the form of things that are pleasing. She looked at Sim in consideration of this, which the doctor rather seemed to see, and with a weary gesture he shook his head.

'I believe that filament may originate in the Almighty,' he said, 'as I told you.' She looked away. 'Such', he said flatly, 'is my Eden.'

'You would have it that I and that horse are of common stock?' The young woman was suddenly all heat and bustle, this anger the more marked as her colour had risen, and he was shocked by the temper in her eyes. She was stiff and brisk in her movements and her pace increased, so that the doctor had to stride out in keeping pace with her. 'You are a bad man, Doctor Sim!'

Sim winced. By her word and manner she meant offence and, indeed, he was offended. In truth, he might have challenged Harewood, had this been wise, but he yet had some self possession.

'I saved George,' he said, 'so bad a man am I.'

Miss Wagstaff stopped and, with Bagshaw passing them,

leading an inquisitive Fanny and looking full forward, she came close to Sim, mollified in some degree. She then subjected him to a searching enquiry, which, when he thought of it, he remembered by her eyes. During the course of this he thought that he saw right to the copper bottom of her. He watched the passage of various thoughts across her face, and then she walked off, without another word, and Sim, who walked immediately after her, was forced to submit to the irritation of polite conversation in the company of the others.

This conversation was of an ordinary milling sort and, as had earlier been the case, the two doctors and Mr Bagshaw were not a good mix. Ordinarily Sim might have enlivened them, but he was not himself. Bagshaw sometimes looked at him but nothing was said, and so the floor was left to Harewood. He was terribly ebullient, but at least he had conversation – and over the next minutes he bestowed this upon them. Chiefly, however, it was directed at Miss Wagstaff and, in the absence of her father, the doctor grew solicitous of her.

'Come this way, Ma'am; you are too near to the horses.' 'Do not stray too far from me, Miss Wagstaff; some of the stallholders look disreputable.' 'Pray lean on my arm, Madam. You need not fear of tiring me. I am sure that I could bear the weight of two of you.' In moving her he forced the other men to follow in their wake, or indeed to make way for them. With a slightly strained smile she submitted to him, for the moment.

'Doctor Sim,' Harewood said. 'Do forgive my enquiry about your motto. I have an idea that you thought I meant to tease you. Nothing could be further from the truth, my dear Sir, I do assure you.'

'Indeed,' replied Sim shortly. He was red under his bushy grey wig with its curls at the ears, and brushed at the sleeve of his coat. Doctor Harewood waited for Sim to compose himself and behave as a gentleman. In truth he was condescending in this, but dressed it up in one or two jocular remarks. Sim said nothing, only bowed; a stiff bow which indicated his mood at that moment. But nothing was actually said.

The more that Harewood detected ill ease about him the more he became sunny, but in general they were quiet, Fanny perhaps excepted, and partly to escape him they began to look round about. All along the course to the start people were beginning to stand at the rails. Coaches had also been drawn up, so that a line of them stretched along the track. Everywhere were people, while on the far side were the tents of the hucksters and traders. Nearer, among the crowd, were performers: a man on stilts – who delighted Fanny – another with a performing dog. Fanny wanted to watch them and so, telling her to be dignified but not pretentious, Bagshaw excused himself and took the girl toward the crowd; but Miss Wagstaff begged to go too, and therefore the whole party, minus Mr Wagstaff, moved off.

It was a small thing that they did in going to the performers, and yet the mood among them was altered by it. Fanny was delighted as the dog danced, let out a peal of amusement and jumped up three or four times. Bagshaw put his hands upon her, but Miss Wagstaff laughed.

'Dear Fanny,' she said, taking the girl's hands. They laughed together, and while the men watched the man with the dog began another tune. It was jolly, too quick for the dog, but the woman swung the girl round, and the two were joined together by their young lives. It was a brief thing. Miss Wagstaff quickly remembered herself, but while it lasted the men looked on amazed. She quickly grew composed and looked round them. Used to being indulged, she expected to be forgiven; indeed, she was more than forgiven. In watching her, Sim forgot himself. The doctor smiled as her eyes made their stop at him, although Harewood was shocked. Such behaviour he did not expect. Idly he wondered whether to mention it to her father, but felt the better of it. Mr Bagshaw, though, was dumbfounded. He quite stared. His fine eyes had a light in them, his cheeks hung in astonishment; so little did he know that a fine lady could be so natural. He had learned something, and he past two and twenty!

Thereafter the group about the dog broke up. After putting money in the old man's hat they wandered some while among the crowds. Behind them drifted Mr Bagshaw and sometimes Jenny felt that he looked at her. He kept away, however: indeed, there was no room for another. In intervals each of the doctors spoke to her. She found herself turning to one and then the other and, on occasion, they spoke at once. This was insufferable and Sim, at last, seemed to realise this. For this reason he decided to go and mingle with the rich people in the paddock. Harewood bowed as the doctor left. Sim met this with a stiff courtesy, then strode off with a deliberate walk.

Doctor Harewood now had the pleasure of seeing that other parasite, Bagshaw, and his brat, leave the scene, a circumstance he had not reckoned upon and was overjoyed to see. Mr Bagshaw had decided to instruct Fanny. Firstly, he wished to expose her to vulgarity. He wanted her to see the greed generated by gambling. He also wished her to notice the disappointment it visited to the many. She was to be sensible of the loss it brought, and realise its potential to ruin. As well as this, Bagshaw schooled her to look at the grossness of those who won. For relief, she was to do arithmetic. If a horse covered so many yards with each stride how many would take it around the half mile course? If a horse were so long how many feet would there be of horses if they stood in line? Could she construe the speed of each winning horse if a mile might be run in two minutes at thirty miles an hour? She must also, despite any excitement, be sure which horse had won in any disputed finish; and so on.

The girl absorbed this, and somewhat unwillingly agreed that she would try to carry it out.

'Even in our pleasures, Fanny,' observed Bagshaw to the sullen and rather displeased girl, 'we must never be forgetful of ourselves. We must, however, as you must know, endeavour to be happy in spite of it.'

The six that had made up the party was therefore reduced to two; only Harewood and Miss Wagstaff remained. She moved into the space behind her, but Harewood moved as she did and the distance between them remained what it had been; indeed it grew rather less. Just then, however, he was distracted. Both he and Miss Wagstaff noticed two poor children looking at a sweet seller. Suddenly Harewood sprang forward. 'Here, gentlemen, are some coins for your disport,' and, saying this, he produced a purse. Briefly he spoiled his gesture by peering inside it with a beady expression; none the less, after throwing two or three coins back, he brandished some pennies with which he furnished the children. It was done, and he returned in triumph to Miss Wagstaff. She watched him narrowly as Harewood returned, wearing a look of infinite goodness. 'Please, do not mention what you have just seen. I hold it as a truth that when one calculates the cost of an act of charity it ceases to be worthwhile at all.'

Harewood went on to refuse to say anything more about his charity for some time. He might have continued to refuse to say anything about it when he was interrupted. He and Miss Wagstaff acquired some guests. Harewood turned round but to see six, seven, ten children. What was a man of his charitable disposition to do? The purse had another outing. With each it became lighter, and the doctor more disagreeable. More children came. He dispersed more money, until a look of white-eyed terror seemed to seize him. It was at this point that he threatened to horse whip them.

His charity, such as it was, deserved better than this and, unfortunately for him, when the children left them he was further exasperated. As the children departed, one of their own party returned. He was dismayed to notice the big form of Sim approaching from the crowd. Harewood audibly groaned.

'Doctor Harewood,' said Sim, after a bow to Harewood and Miss Wagstaff in turn. 'I have just had the honour of conversing with one of your patients, Mr Matthews, who is discussing his symptoms with several farm men and seeking their advice. It seems his complaint is troubling him sorely. I told him that you were here, Sir, and would doubtless wish to succour him. You may find him by the tent, Sir, over on the left, as you look now.'

Sim smiled, and his face was angelic in its good nature: one might see the apples in his cheeks.

'Hummm,' muttered Harewood. He frowned. Under his wig the lines creased across his forehead; his manner suggested that he wished Mr Matthews dead, not better. While Harewood thought, his eyes passed firstly from one to another and his lips twisted, but there was no escape. Mr Matthews paid too well, far too well, for him to be a moment delayed. Indeed, Mr Matthews was the worst hypochondriac in Lichfield and one of the richest. He was also as strong as a bull. The doctor sighed and thanked Sim for his goodness, but Sim would accept no praise. Eventually, like a ghost encumbered with chains, Harewood slouched off, while Jenny and Sim, without speaking, watched him go.

Although Miss Wagstaff did not say anything she rather enjoyed this performance. In fact she had to stop herself from smiling. Sim was such a rogue. He looked at her now with a smile like a hammock, and she, still not pleased with him, could not help but show a flash of merriment, even of wickedness.

'Sim!' came a sudden voice. 'Doctor Sim, come here, Sir. Come here, Sir, I beg you.'

From close at hand came the voice of her father. He wanted Sim away. Sim at once lost his good humour. His face dropped, but he looked round, adjusting his expression as he moved. Now Miss Wagstaff did laugh.

'Away with you, Sir, you are called.'

The doctor, with good manners, left her. He bowed once and turned, and Miss Wagstaff stood and watched him go. It was, therefore, for the first time that she found herself alone. This was a circumstance that should have led her to join Sim and her father, but at that moment Mr Bagshaw approached. He was a little grave, perhaps shy, and the two found themselves in a slightly uncomfortable awareness of each other. Despite this he paid her the honour of a sort of bow. This was almost civility, she thought. Bagshaw was tactful enough not to say that he had been obliged to return. Fanny had asked if Mr Wagstaff, who had won, was not the sort of man whom she had been warned against. Although he refrained from saying this, he did not say anything else either. The far prospect was pleasing to Bagshaw, who saw no reason to speak just because he and this young woman found themselves together. The green meadow and the soft lines of distant trees were occupation for him, but the silence seemed to affect her, who, all her life, had been brought up to please and be gracious.

'Have you no witticisms for me, Mr Bagshaw?' she said. She turned her head to him and smiled, raising her eyebrows.

'I, Madam? Why should I jest?' Bagshaw was confused and sought out her eyes beneath the broad hat brim.

Miss Wagstaff gave her head a little shake. 'You are a most uncommon man.'

Mr Bagshaw was even more confused. By virtue of this he frowned, his brows folded over his eyes and his mouth pugged up, a comical sort of expression; but his eyes retained their good nature.

She looked at him in that disconcerting way of hers, and it was evident that she thought of him and did not disguise it. Bagshaw had no reason to blush and, as she looked at him, he looked at her, by return of post as it were. Her eyes, of course, drew him, greeny brown, with her finely sketched black brows

71

picked out so that one might see each stroke of the brush where they ended near her nose. Bagshaw noticed, forgetting himself, the mix of red and pink in her cheeks and how her mouth had but to lift at the corners to make her whole aspect warm. She drew her mouth downwards a moment now and broke the spell between them.

'Tell me, Mr Bagshaw, given your charitable and kindly habits ought you to extend the same indulgence to yourself?'

'Ma'am?'

'You are so hard upon yourself, Sir. Forgive me.' She shook her head and was done. She had said too much. Bagshaw, however, bade her go on, but she excused herself and would not be drawn. Bagshaw saw how determined she was having decided upon something. He let the matter drop and the two fell into silence; but it became known to them both, by some means, some understanding, which managed to pass between them that they both looked, one with the other, at the colour and bustle of the day about them and beyond to the green miles, to the meeting of the far scene with the sky. Almost as one, too, they looked upwards. The day was fair, but a great billowing topgallant rose away to the north, its edges lit, a great ship moving under full sail.

'I do promise myself some indulgence of the life within me, Madam.'

'I am glad, Mr Bagshaw, and glad to hear you admit it.'

She smiled and he received this like a benediction, but any further response was made impossible by the thunder of galloping horses, in combination with the shouting of Fanny who came up. Bagshaw silenced her with a raised hand, but Sim and Mr Wagstaff were now also approaching. Sim meant to go. At this there was some recollection made of Doctor Harewood. Bagshaw felt it was inappropriate that they should leave without him, and though Sim promised to send the coach back for Harewood, Bagshaw would not go without him. Thus it was that Fanny, in the keeping of Miss Wagstaff, was returned home while Bagshaw remained. A rather stricken Fanny watched him as the coach rolled away, until at last it regained the road and trundled off out of sight.

Chapter 14

A week after the race meeting Sim decided that a visit to the Wagstaffs could no longer be avoided. He was anxious that Miss Wagstaff would be cool, but could not rest thinking that she was at odds with him and wanted to show that he was not so bad a fellow.

In this mood he approached Mr Wagstaff's house, and only when he saw it, with its height and sub-divided windows, did he realise how anxious he was. He so hoped that Jenny would be civil. He swallowed a moment of nerves, pressed on but was interrupted. He had failed to see Mr and Miss Wagstaff. The men acknowledged each other and then he turned to Jenny. It was a pivotal moment, and meant more to him than he had anticipated, but she smiled and gave him her hand. Sim relaxed, but he also noticed something; the old man took a backward step, which he attributed to Wagstaff's pride in his daughter. Sim noted two things more. He was aware that Miss Wagstaff was pale; there was a tired quality about her. Despite this she was lovely. He saw this now more than ever before, or perhaps felt it, one might say.

Sim thought that she coloured under her straw hat, although a shadow was cast on her eyes. He wanted to stoop to see her properly, but her smile was warm as she met him and something of it was to be found in her eyes, so that he was well pleased with it.

73

The old man seemed to think that he might now reintroduce himself and made some remark or other. Sim looked at him as though unaware he had been there. The impression that Mr Wagstaff gave him was that of an elderly, wrinkled gnome in a coat, hat and boots. In fact Sim thought of this longer and more pointedly than was polite. With greater clarity he noticed that Wagstaff's eyes were regarding him closely, but the brown face, with its stubby nose, was as genial and kindly as ever.

'A damnable – excuse me, my dear – a damnable business, Doctor Sim,' said the older man. 'My daughter tells me that you lose trade.'

'The poem, Mr Wagstaff?' asked Sim. 'It was indeed an outrage, Sir. I am obliged that you consider it to be so yourself.'

'What!' The old man's face, already desiccated, appeared to screw up, his bottom lip passed under his upper one and his small eyes became tiny. 'Damned nonsense – sorry my dear – calling you a quack! A quack, Sir, you! I'd whip the fellow who wrote it, thrash him with a dog whip. "Deny your Creator!" You, Sir! It makes my blood boil! You a dabbler, an enthusiast, a mountebank? How may knowledge ever be increased if men are not to experiment? The advancement of knowledge is part of the Divine plan; so may there be increase and a greater share of happiness for all.' He cast about him for a moment as some emotion grew in him. 'Look at my son, growing in strength in the country. If that be quackery then may we have more of it, I am sure, Sir, very sure. Give me your hand, Sir!'

The old man impulsively grabbed Sim's hand and pumped it. Sim could not help but laugh and, throwing his head back a moment, his ruddy, ploughboy's face was immensely cordial.

'I thank you, Sir!' he said, now shaking the old man's hand, so that the two quite struggled with each other. 'You are most liberal, most kind.'

'No, I am not. If I thought it were true I shouldn't have you in the house, Sir, shouldn't have given you the time of day, no matter what you may have done for George.'

This last remark rather took the wind, which had seemed a fair wind, from their conversation.

'I should be sorry for that,' Sim replied.

Sim looked at the old man and realised that he had done

him a disservice, Mr Wagstaff was a man of spirit. He also observed that Miss Wagstaff had grown sombre. It seemed to him that she better understood her father's temper. Sim wondered whether he should try to explain his views. Was it dishonourable to pretend that the poem had utterly misrepresented him? For a moment he chanced Miss Wagstaff's eyes and knew not to say anything more, although he did not like himself for it; but it was expedient.

Thereafter they had a desultory conversation, one of commonplaces, but Sim's mind rested with the thought of his unconventional views and the habit that truth has of coming out. This is especially true when aided by malice, of course; a similar thing may have occurred to Miss Wagstaff. But, at length, Sim initiated a brighter conversation. His companions were intrigued to hear of his new lavatory. Indeed, Sim was so excited about it that Miss Wagstaff, without warning, burst into laughter. Sim stopped immediately. For a moment he strayed towards annoyance, and meanwhile Mr Wagstaff looked so bewildered that he stood with his mouth open. This was enough for Sim: filled with a sense of absurdity, he laughed out loud, joining Jenny, while the old man grew confused and said that sanitation hardly seemed a laughing matter.

When the laughter had run its course Sim did at last describe his lavatory. This done – and beginning once again to grow enthusiastic – he started to explain the idea he had of duplicating the sounds made in speech and reproducing them artificially in a talking machine. Mr Wagstaff was fascinated by this, and Jenny, who already knew of the machine, began to ask questions about the nature of speech and where sounds might be made in the throat and palate.

The doctor was busy in demonstrating these sounds when they were interrupted; his man, Taplin, had come upon them.

'Accident,' said Taplin. Sim stopped mid-sentence and turned. He had been taken unawares. After a moment he nodded and invited Taplin to say more. His servant, long in the face, probably miserable, looked back at him. Sim could barely contain his irritation.

'Tell me!'

'Doctor Harewood. A carriage tumble. Tipped up on the Stonnall road. They've tuck him to Smith's Farm.'

'Yes?' encouraged Sim. 'And is he injured?'

'Yes, Sir.'

'To what degree?'

'Doh know, Sir.'

Mr Wagstaff followed this conversation, and his eyes showed how keenly he listened to it, He also lent forward, grinding his stick into the soil. As if by some trick he was now again the kindly old man whom Sim thought he knew. It was also evident that Miss Wagstaff was concerned for Harewood. As a result she was brief in her goodbye, just catching his eyes for a moment. She seemed mindful of something that only now occurred to him: he was to treat someone who was ill-disposed toward him.

'I must go,' he said. 'Excuse me.'

'Yes,' said the Wagstaffs together. 'Go!'

The life of a country doctor was one spent bumping and jarring along roads that were often unfit for their purpose. In the months of fine weather journeys might be tolerable, but even then they could be uncomfortable; in bad weather they could be dangerous. The constant discomfort of the ruts and holes was bad enough, but in winter a carriage might become stuck in mud, whilst at any time of year there was the danger of axle damage or overturning.

For these reasons Sim had gone on horseback to treat his colleague. This was safer on the rutted road and he made good time. Before long he neared the farmhouse where Harewood had been taken. As the lane turned, on the right he could see a tall, high-shouldered farmhouse, side on, but he made way cautiously. The road had been pitted by farm traffic; mud on the road had set and channels in it, made by carts, began to catch at his horse's hooves. He could easily imagine how Harewood had been tipped up.

He drew very near now. The horse bobbed its head in front and Sim looked over its pricked ears. He was careful, but his mind strayed despite this. He wondered what he might find and what help he might offer. There were many possible injuries in such a case. He might find a fracture, perhaps no more than bruising and shock, or, worst of all, a head injury, a fractured skull, with all the concomitant risk of coma and death.

Sim passed but a few yards more before he was called by one

of the farm workers who had been stationed to look for him.
'Doctor, in 'ere, Master!'

He turned but saw only the retreating back of a man.
Someone else appeared and took his horse's head, and Sim
followed the man, who ran to the farmhouse door, which was
open in readiness. The man stood aside in the doorway and Sim,
knocking once, went in.

There was a brief hiatus once he stepped inside as
impressions crowded him: stone flags, a fire, the smell of
cooking, a woman approaching and, in a chair to his left, with
his head back and one leg raised, the doctor.

'I need no treatment, Sir, I shall tend myself.'

As Harewood said this, Sim spoke to the woman, grey-haired
and respectable, and went to Harewood. He could tell how altered
the doctor was. Sim could see the pain in him, and Harewood's
posture told him much. Sim was moved, as always, in the face of
pain and put aside every thought of acrimony between them.

'Sir!' he said softly, taking to one knee and beginning to
fiddle with his bag.

I should rather a nightsoilman attended me than you,' said
Harewood. 'But for your instruction,' he muttered, 'I have
injured my knee.' This was obvious, as Harewood knew. 'I use
no technical language.'

Sim got to his feet.

'I have also damaged my ribs,' muttered Harewood,
speaking in intervals. 'I know my business so spare me your
ministrations, I shall not require you, horse doctor!'

'I wonder, Mrs Smith,' said Sim, 'if you would leave us,
please?' He was polite, gracious, in saying this, but it was not a
request. 'Should I be gone before you return, thank you for
sending for me. There will be no charge.'

A grateful smile was her response, but the doctor waved her
away. He said nothing to detain her and she was sensible enough
to know that she was not wanted. Harewood, shifting, looked at
her retreating back. The door shut, and the latch dropped and
settled in its gate. Harewood continued to look at the door, but
Sim turned and surveyed him, without embarrassment and with
some distaste.

'I am in no way surprised, Sir,' he said to Harewood, 'that
you scruple to be treated by a mechanic, a dabbler, an enthusiast,

a mountebank. I should as soon let a washerwoman treat me as suffer your care, but you, Sir, are the quack. You may dose yourself as you please. The longer it may take you to recover the better, as I shall be pleased to assume the care of your patients and their fees while you recuperate.'

Sim got up and marched purposefully out of the house. A minute later there was the sound of a horse in motion and he had gone, leaving Harewood to get home as he might.

Chapter 15

Bagshaw was troubled after the race day; he felt that he had become distracted. The bulk of the next few days was given to Fanny. He was frightened of indulgence, not only for Fanny but for himself. Once it took hold where might it end? He pressed on, therefore, and was assiduous.

This meant that Fanny was kept busy, although she did not mind it. Fanny was tough; her life had always been hard, and she withstood all that he asked of her. This made him think well of her, but their relationship was based on more than respect. Bagshaw found that he enjoyed her company. Despite this, he was often alone at night when she had gone to bed, just as before.

On one such evening he spent the time looking into the light of his fire. Beside him, on a table, were papers relating to a gift. Usually he would have put these away: he never reviewed a charitable act, but gave in token of his good Lord. To take pride in it would have been impious.

Had he counted it, however, making one pile of his giving, it would have stood taller than he. One might have thought that this would have given him peace, but he was not at peace. He was unsettled and so, hoping for expiation, he permitted himself to review. A little stone turning might be instructive.

It was not difficult to discover where the cause of his confusion lay, but this made it no less perplexing. Bagshaw had to admit an attraction to the worldly and fashionable Miss

79

Wagstaff. He thought now of her vain and foolish trappings but also of her eyes, which, irrationally, were so appealing to him. She was a Siren but no more than that, and so he thought again of her eyebrows, which arched over her eyes, and the turn of her cheeks down to her mouth and how this puckered at its ends, with his hands tight on the chair's arms and his eyes unblinking in the winking light.

Eventually the fire-dance grew tired and sank in the grate but Bagshaw remained, and breeding, manners and education notwithstanding made a curious grunting noise known as snoring. When he opened his eyes, when the fire was quite out, it was light. He had to think how he came to find himself there, but once he remembered it was time to get up. 'Eyes on the ceiling, feet on the floor' was a law with him, and so he got up, stiffly, and stretched. He was not well rested. For all this, he washed, shaved and dressed afresh and went out early.

The day always began early for the working folk of Lichfield; from a small hour there were workers on the road. Therefore Bagshaw was not alone in being out, and among the people he met was Sim. In fact, Sim had wanted to speak to him; he had a cause to put to him. Bagshaw was still full of this as he wandered rather absently into the Close.

Had anyone seen him at this time they might have thought that he was in drink. He was aimless in his attentions, but at length he approached the Wagstaffs' house. The house backed onto one end of the Close, and over the wall he could see the glitter of water. There were a church and houses beyond, including his own, but he was idling and decided to have done.

His summons upon the door resounded through the house. It was the sort of summons that the Roundheads had made upon the same door, about a hundred and twenty years before. No-one came, however. He knocked again, and his second battering brought a servant. Bagshaw had a mind to barge in, given her expression, but he was shown in, none the less, and asked to wait in a wide, light and pleasant room where he was comfortably seated.

While he awaited the temptress he rehearsed his indifference to the entrance of Miss Wagstaff. He had determined to apply the principle of reason: it was not convenient to be distracted; nor did he enjoy or approve of the vanities of fashion, of which, it seemed to him, Miss Wagstaff was a perfect monster. Therefore he would expose himself to her mischief, conquer and proceed with his business as before.

Had he known it, the object of his thoughts was seated at that moment almost over his head, her visitor having found her unprepared. She struggled in readying herself, in no way helped in this by her father, who still wore his nightcap.

'What does the fellow want? I know it! He has transferred his affections to you. I cannot abide the fellow, but you know that, my dear. As truly as I am a Christian I cannot abide that man.'

Jenny laughed. She, too, was casual. She wore an open gown in silk, with long sleeves, ruffled at the elbow.

'Picture him,' he said, 'his hair like a bundle of rags, dressed in the clothes of a vagabond preacher. You are too good for him!'

'He is a good man, I believe.'

'Hmph!' grunted the old man. His daughter smiled and began brushing her hair.

'Well, I shall try to dislike him,' she said. 'If only he were not so decent.'

'Good girl,' said Mr Wagstaff, missing her irony, 'And the quicker you dislike him the better.'

As they spoke Mr Bagshaw continued to wait in the room under them. By turns he was both impatient and absent. In a moment that Jenny would have enjoyed he attempted to tame his wild hair. He also knocked bits of dust from his clothes and verified a clock by reference to a pocket watch concealed about him.

It was fortunate that he at last found something to occupy him. On the table, just feet away, was the *Gentleman's Magazine*. It was the edition that Sim had encouraged him to read, no less. He noticed it, looked at it and finally descended on it. Soon he was completely absorbed, lying, almost, across the settee, while he scanned the pages in forgetful, nay happy, attention.

In the room above Jenny was now ready to go down, but her father hovered about her. Under the cap his grey hair poked out and his nose shone. He was agitated. 'I cannot go down, make some excuse for me. You may lie as you chose. No, do not lie, I will not have you lie. Tell him that I do not like him, which, after all, is the truth. There, away with you, go on, Madam, go on; do not keep the fellow waiting.'

It was, therefore, but a minute or so more before Miss Wagstaff descended the stairs and made her way into the drawing room where, she quite expected a disgruntled Bagshaw to be awaiting her. Even so, upon the door opening Miss Wagstaff expected some civility, some gambit, some recognition; her surprise, therefore, on seeing Bagshaw recumbent upon the settee was great indeed. She affected some noise and Bagshaw lowered the magazine. He looked at her, then sprang up and brandished every social nicety that he could remember. Miss Wagstaff laughed and directed him to a chair.

'I am sorry to have kept you waiting, Mr Bagshaw. I regret too that my father will not be joining us as he is not yet dressed.'

Bagshaw listened in dreamy disinterest. Then there came a space that she left for him to fill. Any expectation that he would state his business, however, was disappointed. He continued to stand and look at her, so she again begged him be seated and took a chair herself nearby.

'Do I distract you, Mr Bagshaw?' He kept on glancing at the magazine. She was a touch affronted, and made the remark to bring his attention to heel. Despite this Bagshaw continued to glance at it.

None the less, remembering himself, he said how sorry he was to hear that Mr Wagstaff was unwell, then proceeded to talk of the *Gentleman's Magazine*. 'Madam, have you read the comments of "Vesuvius" upon the abominations of the slave trade? Doctor Sim has just brought him to my attention. The fellow is beginning a campaign against the trade and would welcome any help that I can give. I am to write to him the moment that I am home.'

Miss Wagstaff looked to the proffered – waved, no less – copy of the magazine. She had read it, she said, and added that she endorsed every word. Bagshaw smiled; thrilled that she sympathised with his new interest. She was struck that she had seldom seen his smile. The blossoming of his large face, with his kindly eyes and his even and very white teeth, was a marked alteration to his normal front. Thereafter they sat, quiet, while Bagshaw, immensely pleased, brooded quietly in contemplation of her.

Miss Wagstaff was composed and quite patient under this glassy examination. She sat and made small talk, but Bagshaw itched with something to say. 'Wondrous is it that this abuse of human creatures has for so long escaped my attention – I have been too pre-occupied – but now this oversight is remedied how shall I write, cajole, accuse and shame. I shall write to this "Vesuvius", congratulate him and become a willing partner in the smallest part of removing this evil. How my strictures will wing across the country! Did you read, Madam, how human creatures are captured, driven and sold – sold, if you please – and then transported in misery and filth? I had known that vice and wickedness ride many a horse, Miss Wagstaff, but never such a one as this.'

'It is indeed an evil, Mr Bagshaw.'

'Oh, Madam!' Bagshaw took a great draught of air, turning his head a little to the side, almost emotional. 'Your disapprobation of this pleases me, fires me.'

'Can you wonder, Sir,' said Jenny, 'that I, too, find this trade disgusting?'

But Bagshaw ignored this rebuff. Barely did he stop for breath. 'There is work to be done, Miss Wagstaff, such work. I shall write, I shall lobby; perhaps I shall stand for Parliament. But in good time. There is the written word and my pen. What entire and perfect felicity one may find in a life of good works, and such work waits to be done, enough for years, sufficient for me and my partner, my green-boughed shade to labour in selfless service. By what means, by what complacency, may such things be forgotten; how may vanities preoccupy us when such work remains?'

Hardly had he finished in this mighty declamation than he was up. This time he was too preoccupied even to consider salutations, and announced himself off to resume his life of good works, 'heartened, solidified and shored up'.

At the door Bagshaw halted and engaged her in a sunny and invigorating farewell. Miss Wagstaff was taken aback and not a little amused: he, in his dark clothes and with his bible-black hair, his heavy-eyed solemnity, with such a young man's face, was very different to the men who normally called upon them.

'Madam,' he said, as he was poised to leave. He had forgotten something and now remembered it. How in the happiness of his recollection did he glow, and the woman, intrigued, waited on his words, trying in these last moments of their interview not to allow any levity or laughter into her demeanour. 'I have the design of Doctor Sim's contraption for the despatch of bodily wastes. Is that not heartening, Madam? Is that not edifying? I shall introduce it to my estate.'

With a great thump the door closed on Bagshaw, and his shouting voice to the maid was a moment later cut short by the thump of the other door. Miss Wagstaff laughed, and when her father came running down with the poker, alarmed at all the commotion, she laughed out loud and continued chuckling for some while.

Chapter 16

Sim had been right in what he said to Harewood; he did recover many former patients. He was pragmatic about this, bearing no-one resentment, and such was his diligence that his patients soon forgot any reservations they had about him. Many of them were glad to be again under his care.

For Harewood all this was infuriating and he made some effort to correspond with his flock, but to no avail. He had to be patient while his ribs and knee mended, the latter a concern as he thought that he would have a limp. This troubled him, partly because he was active but also because he was vain; the limp would make him appear old. Of late, under the full doctor's wig, his hair had been thinning. He cut it short but hated that it should recede. On occasion he stood without his wig and traced the progress of his hair's retreat. He was also troubled by a pot belly that made him look, standing naked, as if pregnant. He hated this too. He had already tried to dose himself against it, so far without success.

It seemed a short time ago, when he reflected, that he had been a young man on the brink of his career. The years had passed so quickly. This was so much so that, in remembering his wife, she seemed to belong to another time, to a dream or a story, except that her painting remained in his drawing room and her ring was on a chain around his neck. When he thought of her he occasionally felt her loss as sharply as ever, but, despite this, he had recovered. He found this process of healing incredible and more, it intrigued him that he might still love her yet love anew, and he did, most deeply, love anew. His hope of winning Miss Wagstaff was very real. He promised himself great happiness of her. She would be his friend and companion, someone to whom he might come home; someone to provide the children he wanted; someone with whom he might grow old; and someone, more practically, to manage his home. But most of all he loved her, without thought of advantage or gain or rationality of any sort. He loved her. This feeling had grown stronger in him since his accident. Miss Wagstaff, with her father, had been to sit with him more than once. Her nearness infused him with a sense of wellbeing, and even when she left some sense of her remained: something that lingered until the expectation of seeing her again supplanted it.

It was in such a train of thought that Harewood sat, intending to write a letter. The letter was part of his courtship, and he wrote as though his cat courted Miss Wagstaff's cat. This was very clever, except that his cat was disreputable: adulterous, violent, idle and completely irresponsible. In fact, he had already deflowered Miss Wagstaff's cat in the most gratuitous circumstances. However, Harewood took pen to paper.

While he was thus employed one of his servants came to tell him that he had a visitor. He glanced up, asked who it was and discovered, rather unexpectedly, that it was Sim's manservant. One might have thought that this would have surprised Harewood, but he showed no sign of it. He thought a moment and then asked that Taplin be admitted.

'Mind', he said to the servant, 'that you keep this to yourself.'

The servant was left in no doubt that Harewood meant what he had said. Harewood began to hide his poem. Ordinarily he might have said something as his guest came in; his politeness, however, varied according to his company. He did not look up, but busied himself with his papers and read almost an entire letter. Finally he was good enough to remember his guest. He looked up over his papers and studied the older man. Taplin waited. He was content to wait. In this, however, he did not show the least deference, as Harewood imagined. Taplin would

not permit Harewood to humiliate him, and so he would wait as
long as he needed to do so without once allowing Harewood to
diminish him. It was an accident of birth that had made
Harewood his better, and no intrinsic worth. He waited, then,
with his long face composed, his cheeks hanging and his chin
dark with stubble, a gloomy man but attentive. He was wily, too,
and showed just enough respect to the doctor. Harewood took
this as his due, and at last proceeded to their business.

'The doctor is out?' he asked.

'Yes,' said Taplin.

This exchange led to a silence, and Harewood indicated that
Taplin should come nearer to him, away from the door. Finally
Taplin came to sit close to where Harewood had propped
himself up.

'Mr Taplin,' he whispered, 'I should like you to do me a
service.'

The doctor, in saying this, enquired of the older man's face,
but Taplin showed him nothing. From a purse Harewood took
out a sovereign and showed it to Taplin. Taplin remained
impassive, but Harewood noticed the wink of interest in his
green, rheumy eyes and knew that he had him.

'I should be obliged for intelligence of your master –
information – and a report of anything unusual. You must
forgive me, Mr Taplin, I know how it must seem, but I do it for
the best, you may be sure of that. Can you read well?'

'Ah doh care 'ow it is,' said Taplin, 'an' ah con read.'
Harewood wondered if this were the case and Taplin saw this.
'Ah con read sommat of them notes yow was writin' when I
come in, if yow like.' Taplin had seen Harewood hiding
something and knew, full well, that this offer would be
unwelcome; he said it only to embarrass the other man. It
would not be necessary, Harewood said. Thereafter they
looked at each other.

'Will that be all, Master?'

The working man asserted himself; purposefully Harewood
made him wait.

'Yes,' he said at length, 'thank you.' Harewood was slightly
grand as the money passed between them, much to Taplin's
annoyance.

'Say nothing to the doctor,' Harewood said, as Taplin stood

in black outline with the window behind him. Taplin pulled a face, disgusted.

'No,' he said, and catching the doctor's eyes once he was gone.

Chapter 17

By chance Sim had some free time and had retired to his books. The library was light and sunlight dappled the table, making the grain bright and catching bits of dust. As the doctor moved about, his coat, white stockings and yellow waistcoat were vivid.

He sat down, rubbed his hands over a book and threw off his wig. At once he became a young man again: young, handsome, with the colour of a farm worker and two clear eyes. In truth, too handsome, too hale and much too young, it seemed, to be the man that he was. Just then he heard the bell below. He had a visitor.

'Who is it?' grumbled Sim.

'Mr Bagshaw.'

Sim recovered his wig and asked for Bagshaw to be admitted. Soon he could hear his friend on the stairs, and a moment later he met him in the doorway. In every regard Bagshaw appeared to be what he always was. He wore his usual black and had no wig. He was clean shaven and pink clean but Sim could see that he was different. He was careful not to betray this thought, smiled Bagshaw into a chair and waited.

Once Bagshaw was seated Sim returned to his chair. He was easy and relaxed. He asked after Fanny and chatted of this and that and waited, for all this, for Bagshaw to state his business.

'Doctor Sim,' said Bagshaw. The doctor put aside his

chatter as one would put down a book. Bagshaw glanced at the door.

'Go on!' thought Sim.

'I am not sure, Sir,' said Bagshaw looking back, 'that I can continue in my scheme regarding Fanny.'

The chair creaked under Sim. He was surprised. 'How so, Sir?'

Bagshaw looked pained. For the first time since they had met he was shifting and even embarrassed.

'How so?' repeated Sim.

'I have developed an admiration for a young woman.'

'Ah,' breathed Sim. He nodded his head two or three times, a little weary, being told what he appeared to know. He hardly needed to ask the question but asked it anyway. 'Might I ask whom?'

Bagshaw looked up. Sim at once saw the man that he knew. Bagshaw's eyes hardened, and Sim saw the possibility that he would not tell him. Bagshaw, though, was not without insight himself, and he was honourable.

'Miss Wagstaff,' he said.

Sim nodded a slow and tired nod and looked at the table himself, listening but saying nothing. As Bagshaw had nothing to add there was a moment of quiet. The doctor, however, grew a little red under the stock at his neck.

Bagshaw looked across at him, in a knowing, humane way, resigned to the truth and inconvenience of what he admitted. In his innocence he thought that what was said would not encroach upon the friendship between them, but he was wrong.

'How dare you, Sir,' said Sim, looking up suddenly. Bagshaw looked shocked. 'What of Fanny? Fanny!' Sim said this sarcastically as if Bagshaw had forgotten her. 'It would be monstrous to part with her now. She is not a toy to be played with and put aside, or would you return her to the orphanage or apprentice her? Surely not.'

The chair seemed no longer to be comfortable for Bagshaw. He rolled on his great backside and folded his arms. It looked as if he might burst out with something, but nothing was said, although in truth Bagshaw could not have said much. He gulped on his annoyance. Of a sudden Sim sat up. In response Bagshaw straightened in his chair. The two men stared at each other and each plainly considered the other. By and by, one, then the other, sank in his chair and they fell into silence. This went on for some time, but by degrees, as they reflected, they became themselves again, and presently they were also disposed to talk.

'Whatever may occur,' said Bagshaw, 'Fanny will not be returned to the orphanage or apprenticed.'

'No, Sir,' said Sim. 'I might have known.' The doctor felt that he had behaved badly, something that a moment before might have made him behave worse but now depressed him. 'I might have known that,' he said, finding Bagshaw's eyes. 'I owe you an apology.'

The two men made some sort of visual concord over the table top, Sim a little red. 'The truth, Sir,' he said, 'is that I, too, have an admiration for this lady.'

He glanced again and Bagshaw nodded. 'I know.' He smiled a very good-hearted smile, finding some kind of wry amusement in the situation and its impossibility. Given his friendship with Sim, he had to, in conscience, withdraw, although he did not say as much.

The men got up. Sim took Bagshaw's hand and shook it, once more impressed with the goodness of Mr Bagshaw. There was nothing else to say, however, and they hardly spoke when parting; they may not have spoken at all, in fact. The door soon closed upon Bagshaw, and so too, perhaps, upon their friendship.

Chapter 18

When Bagshaw returned from the doctor's he was unsettled and found it difficult to work. He refused to indulge this feeling, however, and began to write, while beneath him, marching back and forth in the garden, Fanny tried to acquire the hardiness of a Spartan.

Beside him the window made a square of light, with rain making the outside colours hazy. The room was dark, made darker by the floorboards and he was glad of the window.

Bagshaw wrote to 'Vesuvius', having before him the *Gentleman's Magazine*, open at the article about the slave trade. He had absorbed this, and now made suggestions of how the campaign might be furthered. He mooted standing for election, offered money and suggested that they write a poem. This, he thought, would prick the conscience more effectively than other means might do.

When the letter was finished he stretched out his legs under the table and smiled. This feeling of wellbeing shocked him and was a joyous thing. He thanked his Creator, but the thought returned to him of Sim. It appalled Bagshaw that he had become so selfish; he had spent his life putting others before himself. Nor did he wish to give way, yet would try to overcome his weakness. It was not his business to be happy but to increase the happiness of others; he had no expectation for himself.

Presently he got up, marched to the door and took to the stairs. After putting on bad weather clothing he joined Fanny in the garden. Fanny was full of confidence now in her protector and went directly to him. She too wore boots, cape and hood, but she was very wet. Bagshaw was mindful of this and frowned at the rat's tail hair.

'Do not get cold, child.' He tried to be stern but his eyes were full of warmth. Looking down at her he struggled to hide his affection for her but he allowed a compliment to escape him. 'You have shown great fortitude, I am pleased, Fanny.'

She smiled and cheerfully began walking again, now with Bagshaw beside her, the two swinging their arms like soldiers.

The position that he chose for their marching was one that was open to the road; something that he anticipated would encourage rudeness from that quarter. Indeed, he almost meant to induce it. It was an important lesson for Fanny that she must learn to ignore what was impertinent and not be deflected by it. Therefore the two continued for some time, tramping up and down, and hardly hearing one or two cat-calls, until Bagshaw, who waited for a signal from the house, thought that they had done enough. Fanny complained of taking cold, but he dismissed this and they marched another two or three minutes.

Bagshaw had ensured that they returned to hot baths. Fanny was despatched into the care of the housekeeper whilst he retired to his study. He had obtained a great bath and this was waiting for him, steaming, the last buckets just being added. Once in the privacy of the study Bagshaw undressed and sank into his bath, only his shaggy head rising from the water, save for one hand, with a book in it. A fire in the grate kept the temperature up. In short he was comfortable, but he was not happy, thinking once again of Miss Wagstaff and Sim. None the less, he was some while in his bath. He eventually rose, dripping, and determined upon dinner.

Upon entering the drawing room Bagshaw took his book to a chair near the white fireplace. Fanny was already there, reading. Her long hair was drying now; idly Bagshaw noticed how it began to regain its rich colour. She looked up as he entered and her smile caught him unawares; he responded spontaneously and, in doing this, betrayed his affection for her. This would not do; he quickly hid it. But the girl was satisfied and turned as before to her book, warm, happy and secure by their fireside.

Since Bagshaw was a fair man, and had only a small staff, he was patient waiting for dinner. It was some time before he and Fanny sat to eat, and very ready were they to enjoy it, but then the evening, which had pleasantly run along its course, began to take an unpleasant turn. Bagshaw, enjoying his food, was slow to realise that Fanny was not eating. When Bagshaw chided her she began again, but did not eat for long and soon afterwards Fanny begged to be excused.

Bagshaw was hungry but put aside his utensils. He waved a hand, allowing her to move, which looked unkind but was not meant as such. While he watched, Fanny crept to a chair where she shifted, turning from one position to another.

Mr Bagshaw was appalled by this turn of events. He was not entirely sure what to do, and began to blame himself for exposing her to the rain. He was usually so decided in his actions, but as he rubbed at his hands and glanced about him, the white about the eyes, which was picked out in the firelight, said much about his uncertainty. Suddenly he got up and strode over to her. She responded as he spoke to her, guilty that she caused him any trouble or anxiety; she even raised her head and made an attempt at perkiness. Mr Bagshaw shook his head and wished that he could believe her. Before long, too, she gave up this attempt. She let her head sink against the arm of the chair and begged just a few minutes' peace. Bagshaw knelt beside her, running the back of his fingers against her cheek. Already he was pondering whether he could trust Harewood or not.

Chapter 19

Thus Sim, who had not expected to hear from Bagshaw so soon, found himself summoned to Bagshaw's house. The two men met in the doorway, and how strange it was: something was changed between them. Each took stock of this for a moment, then they turned to the business at hand.

Unknown to Mr Bagshaw, Sim was now very tired. He had come from a woman having a difficult labour and his exertion had been considerable. However, he had saved her, and the child, and this was his reward, as the family could not pay him.

Although he was exhausted, it was interesting to watch Sim once he came within reach of the sick room. He was like an actor upon the boards; his weariness seemed to leave him. His manner too bespoke confidence, matter-of-factness. He also exuded a deep compassion, which Bagshaw, watching, noticed. Sim was moved to see Fanny ill and ran the back of his middle fingers down her cheek. Everything he did suggested that he thought only of her, and he smiled with real pleasure as she responded and was so obviously glad to see him. Thus, his tiredness thrown off like a coat, he gave every scrap of attention to her. While Bagshaw came and went, pacing to and from the bed, Sim began to administer to her, and hardly knew that Bagshaw was there.

The intimacy of the scene about the bed was made the greater as the light was fading outside. Gradually the room contracted around them, although the doctor seemed not to notice. He was absorbed in trying to reduce her temperature. He called for water and a towel and laboured to bring it down. By turns, as she looked at him, his features softened, and sometimes he smiled and say something to her. Before long they had to have candles lit, although the firelight provided some light – in which Fanny's winking eyes were occasionally caught, seeking out Bagshaw as he looked at her and sometimes as he was bent over the bed. He was sick with worry but hardly knew how to express it, and soon returned to the chair by the fire, where he sat with his bulk hunched into a very small compass.

In the firelight one might see the needles of self blame in Bagshaw, but he also thought of something else. He was troubled that he could be so affected yet struggled to express it. Was that not a most unnatural thing, and what did it say of him? He was so much preoccupied in his thoughts that he did not even hear the bell downstairs. For this reason he was shocked, even affronted, when Bingley, the butler, entered the room without, it seemed, any cause.

'Miss Wagstaff,' said Bingley. She had discovered their business when her father had called on Sim in hope of finding a partner for cards.

Bagshaw did not immediately comprehend what was said to him. Bingley was obliged to repeat himself.

'She begs to come in, Sir,' said Bingley. 'She is most insistent.' Bagshaw took an age to digest this information but, at last, he nodded.

So it was that Miss Wagstaff was added to their number, and notwithstanding their earlier conversation she was not entirely welcome. Each man looked at the other as they listened to her progress up the stairs. Suddenly she came in with great energy and bustle. Bagshaw scrambled to his feet.

Each of the men made a proper recognition, even Bagshaw, who was not good at such things, and even Sim, who was busy. For her part she was polite, but the salutations were necessarily short. She came in with her colour up from her swift walk, dressed in a cape over a plain skirt. She wore a cap on her hair, which was gathered, and her dress exposed her white arms, almost to the elbow, as if she came to work.

'Forgive me, Mr Bagshaw, I do not mean to intrude. I come to help, if I can.'

Her utility or otherwise was not a matter for Bagshaw and he looked to the doctor. The doctor raised his head and straightened, unravelled, one might say. They watched him and then Bagshaw watched her. She approached Sim as if to lift a hand to the shadows under his eyes.

'You are tired, Sir.'

'Mrs Clifford.'

'How is she?' she asked. 'I heard that the midwife sent for you.'

'Recovering,' said Sim. 'As is the child.'

Jenny absorbed this information as if she had expected worse news, and it seemed to be a great relief to her. She began to busy herself, but then looked again at the doctor. She weighed his tiredness against the fact that the Cliffords were penniless. While this thought was in her mind she bestowed on him a look, a sort of benediction, a slow-burning warmth, like that of embers sinking in the grate. It was but a moment then, seamlessly, she had taken his place. The doctor still basked in the glow of it and did not immediately realise that she had moved. He felt Bagshaw's eyes upon him, but Jenny's attention had shifted, and though Sim was not forgotten he was now superfluous. Now it was Fanny's turn, and Bagshaw noted how she responded to Jenny. While the men watched, Jenny tended her: among the pragmatic things, the dabbing with the cloth, for example, she was motherly. Once, bending down, she placed her head against the girl's cheek. The doctor frowned at this, but Miss Wagstaff thought only of Fanny. She became forgetful of them, in fact. Only when Fanny closed her eyes did Jenny let the invalid's head sink onto the pillow before she rose and smiled. The men waited, seeing that she meant something. On the lace of her rustling dress she had vomit and, holding up a hand, she signified that she also had it there. She took up a cloth, wiped her fingers and shrugged. She wore it as if it was lavender water. It was then, seeing the sick on her, that Bagshaw knew that he wanted her; but what of Sim? What of Sim? Bagshaw, sickened with worry as he was for Fanny, felt himself drunk with too much feeling. Sim, meanwhile, decided to be gone. The crisis was over, at least so far as Fanny was concerned. There was no need for him to be there, at least for the present; and with a word to Fanny, who shook his big hand, and Miss Wagstaff, who looked up to rest her eyes on his a moment, and to Bagshaw, to whom he spoke of Fanny as they tramped down the stairs, Sim left them, leaving them to each another.

Chapter 20

A day or so later Bagshaw sat in his study, with the square window beside him spattered with rain. The rain reminded him of Fanny, but she was growing better, for which he praised the Almighty. He was also mindful of the part that Sim and Miss Wagstaff had played. Jenny was coming that hour to see Fanny, but he would keep away. He and Jenny had exchanged differing views about fashion. This had occurred when she had promised Fanny a dress and Bagshaw objected. Jenny had said that fashion added to her pleasure, and was it always sinful to seek out pleasure in life? She realised that she wasted her breath in saying this to him, and indeed Bagshaw had not been sympathetic.

Aside from their cross words he was not without another reason for keeping away. There was no doubt now; he was convinced of his feelings for her. On one hand this thrilled him, but he was ashamed to fail with Fanny and guilty at seeking to come between her and Sim, so struggled with himself and kept away.

It was well that he found distraction in writing to his new friend 'Vesuvius'. He scratched out, 'My dear Vesuvius, Sir' on a piece of paper, then flopped back in the chair. From the chair he might watch for Jenny, but he tried not to think of her. Therefore he took the quill and tickled at the end of his nose, trying to edit a poem that Vesuvius had written.

In beach-fringed vegetation,
Near vulgar habitation,
He arms to save his nation,
But rues his noble station,
When captured by the press!

Bagshaw wished extraordinarily to be kind to this, but did not like it. It would not do. Rather more, he thought, the poem should take the form that he had determined:

By baking Afric's rolling tide,
Come men with dogs that all need hide
Who bear the tint of sable shade,
Though all by one Creator made.

This, thought Bagshaw, was much better. None the less he was good enough to suggest that they meet, if 'Vesuvius' did not like it, and indeed otherwise, and invited his friend to come to Lichfield.

He went on with his letter but was frustrated, just then, in his firm intention of completing it. Down below, on the drive, he detected the arrival of Jenny. Unable thereafter to write another word, he put down his pen, scrambled to his feet and watched her until her foolish hat passed from view. Jenny weighed only about nine stones, but he followed her progress from the hall up the stairs. Fleetingly he heard her weight on the boards outside his door, but he recollected himself. He was ashamed to stand spying at the door. Resolutely he returned to his letter and paid not the slightest heed when Jenny left some time after. None the less, he had come to a decision with regard to her. For a moment he lifted his head as he considered it, then looked down and went on as before.

Miss Wagstaff was next expected at the house on the following day, and on the morning of that day Bagshaw was once more in his tub. The water was cold, and only exercise of considerable will kept him, as he was, up to his neck in it.

About him the study was well lit and there was a wash of light in the room that picked out the grain of the wood and the colours of the book spines. This room was Bagshaw's

100

favourite. It afforded him privacy and opportunity to think of other things apart from the responsibility of his adoptive parenthood. (As he thought of Fanny now he once more gave thanks for her continuing recovery.) He also thought of Jenny, as he did sometimes in passing, and then with a great whoosh pulled himself up out of the tub. He was revealed as a young man of considerable musculature. The water shone on his thick pectorals and found the turn of his shoulders and biceps in catching the light. Bagshaw, as if shy, was soon drying himself, the muscles quivering in his brisk sideways motion.

When the towel was discarded it was time for him to dress. On the floor, in a neat pile, were his clothes, and he crossed the bare boards and picked them up, gingerly: impeccable underclothes, stockings, but something else. There was something very strange about this: yellow breeches, a waistcoat of glossy satin, crossed with blue, a coat in plum and a fine quality shirt.

The man who some minutes afterward took to the stairs was a splendid creature; and this without his hat, which remained in its box. He also lacked his cane, snuff box, chain, watch and, something more, his perfume. To his eternal shame he had also purchased perfume: oh, the humiliation!

In balance, however, one might say that the plum coat was a great success, one he had obtained, with great fortune, ready made. The shoulders were full and crisp and the tails hung down nicely, just where his stockings covered his well-turned legs; and happy, striking, was the contrast of the breeches with the plum coat. From the front the waistcoat also complemented coat and breeches alike. He was magnificent.

While Miss Wagstaff's opinion was most crucial, it also remained to be seen how other people would react to this alteration. He had an early trial of this. Just then, as luck would have it, Bingley came onto the landing. He opened his mouth wide at the sight of Bagshaw, and half said something. He stared. Bagshaw lumbered past him as if he were a bull that had gone through a washing line and carried someone's fineries on its horns. He would have told Bingley to mind his own business but was altogether too distracted. He could think of nothing but Miss Wagstaff. Fashionable or not, he knew her merit. For this reason he was sure that she would want him, a man rooted in unchanging values; a man of parts; a man like an oak, under whose far-reaching boughs she might find shelter from sun or rain. More than this, however, she had taught him something. He might be happy as well as good, and happiness was not a chimera but could be attained if she would, as he fervently wished, but accept him.

At last he stood outside the door. On the other side of it he could hear her voice. After a moment Bagshaw knocked briskly and strode in. The girl and the woman looked round, each one breaking off in what they had been doing, and the reaction of each was marked. Fanny, facing him, saw him first. She had, until then, been lying back against her pillows. She began with the makings of a smile at seeing him, then dropped her chin as her eyes widened. At once she knew the meaning of this. She coloured, and the water rose in her eyes; none the less she settled to watch. Miss Wagstaff turned slowly, with the measured politeness with which she had been brought up. Like Fanny she began with a smile, but stopped short. Her eyes, once they found him, spread like ink drops on a blotter; her 'Good morning' became a herring bone in her throat.

For the first time Bagshaw felt something like regret. He was embarrassed; he had been heady. He rather thought that he coloured. He could see that Miss Wagstaff also saw the full meaning of it, but the die was cast. He must go on; he had no choice.

'Miss Wagstaff. Might I have the honour of speaking with you privately? Excuse us, Fanny.'

Fanny scowled, bull-doggy, cross to be excluded, although Miss Wagstaff seemed to have no wish to leave her. Indeed, if occupation or excuse had presented itself Jenny would have remained where she stood. Bagshaw was laughable now; he forgot he had not yet asked his question, or had it answered as he would wish, and in his honesty he dropped the disguise that manners and convention put in his way, so that he looked at her as the great prize she was to him. Without embarrassment he studied, as he had often wished to do, her brows and dark eyes, and her face was like a new-found land to him. But for want of his proposal he might have lifted a hand and traced it, in its rises and falls and all that made it what it was, but this business stood between them. He was breathless and impatient as he opened the door; indeed, it seemed that he had fleas about his linen as she hesitated. It was all he might do not to hurry her; however, after a moment she stepped out, looking to the boards and deep in thought. Bagshaw at last had her to himself. He collected himself, but was heady and forced to steady his breathing. Behind the door Fanny took station, pressing her ear hard against the wood.

'My dear Miss Wagstaff, my dear, dear Madam.' He grew wet about his eyes and she noticed this. There was a great sincerity in him, which spoke well of him. Mr Bagshaw was like a ship that began to fail for lack of wind, but Miss Wagstaff would have had a stony heart not to be moved. Above the great chops Bagshaw had fine eyes, and the white light in them was kind and, above all, passionate. She could not help but be touched. It was for only a moment that Bagshaw was confused, but it seemed a long time and patiently she smiled for him, waiting while he mouthed and flapped. Bagshaw was confused whether to speak his mind or heart, but at length he made a great effort, pressed his hands together and spoke. 'My dear, dear Madam, will you please . . .'

The door knocker sounded below them. Bagshaw was quite shaken. Jenny, who had hung upon his words, coloured and let out a short puff of air.

'Marry me,' said Bagshaw, rather flatly.

Miss Wagstaff, although she had known for the last two or three minutes that this was coming, was immensely moved, and the water rose in her eyes. Bagshaw waited in trepidation but already the slow tread of Bingley was making its way up the stairs. Within a moment he had become visible; a creak, a heavy tread, a moment more and he spoke.

'The doctor, Sir,' he said, peering up at them. Bagshaw sighed, putting his full weight upon the banister, but the moment was gone. He looked at Bingley and nodded, and Bingley began the slow tramp down again.

'I shall wait to hear,' said Bagshaw. Miss Wagstaff nodded and then Bagshaw dropped heavily onto the stairs. Bump, bump, bump, and he was gone. She remained a moment or so where she was, sunk in thought.

Bagshaw met Sim on the lower steps. The doctor, young in his bushy-eared wig, big in his long coat, with its white shirt cuffs frilled at his hands, stopped as Bagshaw met him.

The two men met: how inadequate it is to say this! They collided, one might say; the one, Bagshaw, appeared like an apparition before Sim. What a proud man Bagshaw was, however; he hated his new clothes, but made no apology for himself. Without a word being said, he passed into an adjoining room. After a moment Sim straightened from his own bow, looked towards the door whence Bagshaw had gone and considered the matter. He was amused and he was shocked and he was wry. He knew the significance of what he had seen. He was not unconcerned too and for a moment he was ironic, but he was worldlier than Bagshaw and forgave him his about turn. Sim looked once more to the door and some thought passed across his face; but he must get on. Curious and anxious as he was, to some extent, he began his own tramp up the stairs. Neither he nor Miss Wagstaff nor even Fanny said a word of what they had seen.

Chapter 21

After the proposal Miss Wagstaff stayed to speak to Sim, and stood to watch while he examined Fanny; but the doctor was inhibited, as Jenny was herself, and even Fanny knew better than to mention the spectacle that they had seen. It was a strained examination, and Sim failed in making merry that she was better. He was not himself, and Fanny noticed how ill at ease they both were. Once Sim had made his diagnosis Miss Wagstaff left. He bowed her out, and it seemed to Fanny that the doctor knew all that had occurred. Soon afterward he also left himself.

Once they were gone Mr Bagshaw reappeared, but he was not himself either. He was out of sorts in his outfit and jangled with an excitement that Fanny had never seen in him before. Mr Bagshaw was distracted, but he realised that Fanny had been unsettled. In consequence he decided to tell her about his proposal. Although he had intended to wait for his answer before he told her, he determined to do so immediately, since her life would be changed by it almost as much as his own. For this reason he approached her room and knocked softly on the door. He was obliged to knock more than once but, at length, she opened it. Fanny had her bucket in her hands. She had anticipated being required to fetch water for washing and was ready, as she did not wish to be asked to do it and still less told to do so.

'Fanny,' said Bagshaw. She raised her eyes to look at him, her face deadpan. 'I have something to tell you. I have asked Miss Wagstaff to be my wife.'

'I know,' replied Fanny. That said, she said nothing more and her expression did not alter.

'Are you not pleased?' asked Bagshaw. For a moment he rested a hand on a hip, something oddly fitting to his dandy clothing. Fanny noticed this. 'We shall be a family.'

'You will not send me back to the orphanage then?'

'No!' said Bagshaw, shaking his big head. 'No. How can you ask that, Fanny? Do you not know me better than that?'

'You are changed.' She was deliberate in saying this. She knew that she would prick him. She saw in his eyes that he felt this, but she wanted to hurt him. She felt a number of things, some of which she could not articulate, but she knew that she felt disappointment. 'Then I can have ribbons now, can I?' she asked.

Bagshaw detected sarcasm and was wounded by this. He looked at her and could see that he was right; her brown brows framed it with the niceness of a Drury Lane actress. He was very hurt.

There was a gap of some seconds and neither spoke. 'You need not wash in cold water this morning,' he said at last, almost as if he tried to re-establish some authority. 'I shall bring some hot water to you presently when it becomes available.'

Something of her wanness left her on Bagshaw saying this. Her eyes became softer and dropped. After a moment she looked from the floor and the two exchanged something, he imagined, of a tacit understanding. Despite this, while he remained in the doorway she thanked him for his care of her and, begging to be excused, gently closed the door in his face.

So it was that he came to be cast out, rather in the manner of a child who had been excluded from a room, but he kept his word about the water. After washing she received her morning's work, and he retired to his study. Bagshaw sighed as he closed the door behind him but he wanted to be private; only in his own company could he make sense of the different thoughts within him. He also wished to hide his excitement. His high station in the study allowed him to savour this; from the window he might watch the path that would bring his answer.

In fact, Bagshaw's vantage point allowed him to do more than watch the path; he was able to see the Wagstaffs' house. As he looked he sometimes found himself drawn to his own reflection, which gazed back at him. As he stared he considered himself. Firstly he was embarrassed; he had seen how people looked at him. He recognised the self-regard that had brought him to this and could not help but be ashamed of it, realising the pride he had always taken in rising above self.

He sighed as he thought of Fanny's disappointment in him. He realised how much he cared for her good opinion, and that of Sim, upon whom he had stolen a march. But, ashamed or not, he had acted upon a sudden happiness that had slipped its hand into his. For his sake, who surely was not so bad a fellow, he could not act otherwise.

Mr Bagshaw had no idea how long he might be called upon to wait. He sat out his vigil, though; sometimes looking from the window, sometimes at the big face looking back at him. At one point he even smiled, amused by the excitement in him, the breathlessness, the quickening of his heart: he had never been a lover, rather one who stood and watched, on the outside looking in. But here he was, and the waiting, while intolerable, was at the same time exhilarating; and so he sat and pressed close to the glass.

If an answer from Miss Wagstaff had not come within two, three or more hours Bagshaw would still have remained where he was, but before long he recognised one of the Wagstaffs' servants. He became unsettled until finally she came hurrying up the drive; at once he leapt up, scrambled across the floor and began to tumble down the stairs, but he stopped himself. He would keep his dignity.

Behind her door Fanny waited too and, as she listened, she heard his tread begin again.

'Bang, bang, bang' came the summons at the door. It too came again, in short succession. Bagshaw called that he would answer it, and his tread passed her and continued on its way to the front door.

He was kind to the woman who stood red-faced, glowing like an oven-warmed pie. He smiled for her and was patient as she made a great fuss of handing over her note, but at last she was finished. He gave her a coin and blessed her and, standing with his back to the door and with his heart pounding, read the reply.

> My dear Mr Bagshaw,
> I leave for Rugeley with my father and Doctor Harewood at 11 and but for this would have come to speak with you, not thinking it proper to write what ought to be said directly. Such is my esteem for you that I wanted to reply in person but, knowing that you waited for an answer, have written as you see.
> I cannot marry you, my dear Sir. I am thankful, nay moved, by your attention to me. I know you, Mr Bagshaw, for a good man, but I cannot marry you as, for all my warm regard, my feelings for you do not permit it.
> I am grieved to tell you this but hope that any pain which may be caused you will be of short duration, and we may again resume our valuable and decent friendship as before.
> I am, Sir, with the deepest gratitude and good wishes, your friend, Jenny Wagstaff.

Bagshaw grew heavy and rather tired as he read this, crumpled the paper and dropped it, although, thinking better of this, he stooped down and retrieved it. He found some place for it about him, sank back and, as if he might make it all untrue, closed his eyes. He did not know that he had done it, but he said something. Like a ghost, Fanny crept forward and watched him, in pity, but fascinated. As she watched he bent forward and turned up a rear like a cart horse's. Mr Bagshaw looked, closely, at his revolting breeches and became angry.

In the contemplation of his legs at close quarters he began to think of his other silks, fripperies and fineries, and bending down, as he was, his face became brick red and his weight drew his cheeks out. Thus he considered himself and grew more and more irritated. Had he not prostituted himself? For this reason the clothes he wore became intolerable to him. In fact, all his disappointment became vested in them, and so he determined upon a desperate course of action.

Thus it was, still wearing his fine raiment, that Bagshaw found himself on the path that led from his home. He passed the stub tower of St Chad's Church and marched along the glittering Stowe water. To his front the city grew near. In the ups and downs of its roofs and chimneys it ran crosswise before him. In another mood the cathedral, on his right, might have seemed like a flower, like a crocus. Today it looked like an old church with more spires than it needed. He thought only of its rear and, in particular, the house where the Wagstaffs had their home.

It was now near eleven, but in time he entered the Close, passing through the gate. He slipped between the buildings on either side, and round the angle of the wall saw that the Wagstaffs' carriage was still there.

The walk from his home had quickened Bagshaw's breathing. Leaning against a mossy wall he recovered himself, and took opportunity to think. When he was ready he tiptoed along the corner wall and took up his position. He hoped that they would not be delayed; any delay might give time for reflection and he did not wish to reflect. He drew his meaty frame from view, but hardly had he settled than the party left the house and began to make their way toward the carriage. He let them come closer. They approached, walking an idle, everyday walk, quite unprepared: Miss Wagstaff and Harewood, and Mr Wagstaff in front.

'You see, Madam, what I think of these trappings!' Bagshaw seemed, as it appeared to the party, to have come from the very ground, and, having said this, marched up. Not only this: he had his breeches undone! Let it be said that he wore some species of underwear as, with abandon and hopping about, he pulled off his fine silken breeches and waved them above his head. Thereafter he fell upon them with his teeth.

'The man's mad, Harewood!' The old eyes of Mr Wagstaff, which sometimes appeared lost among the folds and wrinkles of his face, now opened wide, as did his mouth. The old man staggered and then adopted a fighting pose. He did, in fact, land one or two blows on Bagshaw, who ignored him and beat him off with his breeches. 'Damnation!' shouted the old man. 'Sorry, my dear,' he remarked, looking to Miss Wagstaff and speaking in quite another voice. Harewood tried to restrain him, but the old man hit him. Running back to Miss Wagstaff, Harewood threw a shawl over her head. She threw this down, and when the doctor attempted to cover her eyes she knocked his arm away. She looked round him, and watched with great interest.

'Spare us your member, Sir!' implored the doctor.

Bagshaw was now ripping the breeches with his hands, having failed, even in his passion, to destroy them with his teeth. This done, he ripped off his waistcoat. The glossy satin of its yellow cloth was vivid as he held it up; it too was torn up. He began on his shirt.

Before long Bagshaw was quite naked, save for a small covering around his hinder parts. He gesticulated, jumped up and down and repeatedly picked up the bits of cloth, only to throw them down again. Once in triumph, as the carriage was rolling, he dared the eyes of Jenny: never, never, never, however, never, if he lived to be a hundred and one, never, never, never would he understand these damned creatures, women! They confounded him, and thus in consternation he looked to Jenny, who laughed. She laughed at him. He was tormented by one last exhibition of the dark eyes, and then he was left, all but naked, standing in the road as the carriage gathered speed, the coachman flailing the poor horses as if wolves pursued them, and three heads projecting from the windows, looking back at him, until the whole disappeared from sight.

Chapter 22

The doctor mounted the stairs with mixed emotions, as he had heard by now of Miss Wagstaff's refusal of Bagshaw and what, of course, had happened after it. Sim was glad that she had refused him, but he felt for Bagshaw all the same.

The effort of climbing the stairs was displeasing to Sim. He had that day been kicked by a horse, which had bruised him. His face was flushed, contrasting with his wig and making incongruous his heavy clothing, which was that of the road.

Behind him, Fanny crept up, peering round him very furtively, although the doctor bumped up the stairs and quite announced his coming. At length they stood outside Bagshaw's panelled door. The doctor knocked: no answer. The doctor knocked again.

Presently a voice within asked who it was, although Bagshaw knew who it was perfectly well. He was rude, asking to be excused as he was not well. Those with his interests at heart could not neglect him, though, and Fanny would not. It had been she who had called Sim, and quite properly as he had assured her.

Bagshaw had now been unwell for a week, ever since his return from Mr Wagstaff's home. For some days he had not left his bed, and though Fanny had approached he had always sent her away. However, finding that he had acquired black treacle –

one of Bagshaw's own remedies – she had waited no longer. Hence she (and the doctor) now demanded entry.

At last a key turned. Fanny rushed in and found Bagshaw shuffling to his bed. He turned as the door opened and his eyes widened at the impropriety of being caught in his nightshirt. (He had a nightcap on too, which ended in a pom-pom down his back.) Thus he sprang into bed as if a mouse had run up his leg. Once there, he scowled at Fanny fiercely.

Sim came in, his high colour making his eyes bold. His look of disapproval was very marked, and would have been more so had he realised that the window was open. He frowned at the board floor, and the bed with its canopy which was heavier clad than Bagshaw. All seemed so austere.

The doctor had expected to be the central figure, but found that Fanny had upstaged him. While Sim prepared for the examination she scolded Bagshaw and brought a chair to the bedside, but Sim only pretended to be unready. He saw that Fanny needed to reassure herself. He was touched too to see the feeling that had grown between them, which excluded him; and Sim noticed that Bagshaw, when Fanny impulsively took his hand, delayed before removing it.

Given his weight loss, Bagshaw had contracted, and it was almost a handsome frame that had settled on his face. He would soon, all in all, be a fine, handsome creature, as the doctor, in reasserting himself, observed; but he noticed also that Bagshaw was mightily pale.

The tryst between Bagshaw and Fanny was broken at last by the doctor. By means of a soft cough he intervened, and Fanny was ousted from her chair. The doctor smiled but she became fractious, turning impudent eyes on him. Bagshaw made appeal, while Sim, still patient, again smiled her away. Finally Bagshaw was left with his physician and erstwhile friend.

'A bitter pill for you,' said the doctor, lifting his brows and finding Bagshaw's eyes. The two men understood each other. Bagshaw nodded. Perking up, he tried for stoicism.

'I should have known. I was a fool, but I wish you well of her. You heard of how I came to walk home in my linen?'

'Yes!' chuckled Sim. 'Several times. The town is still talking of it.' He threw his head back and laughed, such a natural laugh and his eyes so warm that Bagshaw was reminded of his liking for him. 'Thus you came to be ill as you now are. Mr Wagstaff fears for your sanity.'

Bagshaw smiled. 'I am sick at heart.' The doctor looked at him, and dropped heavily and intentionally onto the bed, his weight knocking Bagshaw from his thoughts.

Sim's face became composed, and sombre. 'It is past! Now, Sir, treatment, renewed vigour of life and out once more into the many-coloured day.' He put a hand on Bagshaw's arm and gave it a little shake, finding his patient's eyes and nodding.

Bagshaw seemed to accept his words. 'I betrayed your friendship,' he said, taking his eyes off to some bleak corner. 'I thought only of myself.'

'No,' said Sim. 'The lady is no more mine than she was yours. She is a free agent and you did well to think of yourself. It is not always culpable, my friend, to pursue your own happiness.'

Bagshaw at last nodded, and the two men looked at each other.

'Now,' said the doctor, a light in his eyes, 'for your recovery and a resumption of life.'

So it was that Bagshaw was preserved, once more to take his place in the many-coloured day. His treatment began forthwith; the treacle was thrown from the window, and all was done that was requisite; although it was Doctor Commonsense who proved most useful of all. Thus Sim told the lady of the house that Bagshaw would not die and, invested with plenipotentiary powers, Fanny began to supervise his recovery. (Indeed, she had run the household since Bagshaw withdrew. The servants knew better than to dispute her authority; they knew their master better. She had managed things very well, too.)

None the less, it was a further three days before Bagshaw again came to the lower part of the house. It was already evening and he did not stay long, not wishing to parade his tiredness and melancholia before Fanny. Much, however, had he wanted to be part of the life and times of the house, and he looked forward to the daylight of the morrow.

During his illness Fanny had grown accustomed to using Bagshaw's chair, by the fire and on the side away from the windows, but she waited for him to notice before she moved; then, pointedly and delightedly, she gave way. When this was done she took her place and, as was their custom, they sat out the dying of the light. Bagshaw being in his chair and she in hers encouraged her to think that he would talk, as he generally did; but he was quiet and did not seem to wish to converse, and so they sank into a sort of seclusion, brought, in part, by the closing of the outside light about them.

The light from the fire caught the dead, unwinking eyes of Bagshaw, illuminating the large whiteness of his eyes, the flat of his brow and the turn of his cheekbones; drawing attention, Fanny thought, to some want in him that she could not supply. Sometimes, too, he was caught by great fits of coughing, and heaved.

Occasionally, though, he acknowledged her. His great face turned to her and he asked after something, her reading or some such thing, or else he said something weighty or pleasant and her eyes, meeting his, warmed. In such an interlude Fanny recalled two letters that had come for him while he was unwell and that she had kept aside. She produced these now, rather shyly, thinking that he might be annoyed by her delay, but Bagshaw perked up and thanked her gravely. Fanny gave her burnished head a little shake, as she sometimes did when the mood caught her, and Bagshaw ripped open the first envelope, turning the page to the light.

The Close, Lichfield

Sir,
        You may discern by the shakiness of my hand the shock that I received by your frolic of yesterday. Pray also conceive the difficulty Doctor Harewood had in relieving my distemper when his hand shook as much as my own. Frankly, Sir, do I own the fear that I entertained of your member. Understand, however, that I had no misapprehension of it for myself but for my horses. Imagine the commotion that must have ensured had you utterly forgotten yourself: my two bay mares may have taken fright and run mad through the streets, but more than this, have you considered the mischief that must have been visited upon my daughter, and indeed to any other female who happened to come upon you? It will not do, Sir! I am a man of the world but I could only eat one piece of pie that

evening and quite paled at the thought of dessert.

I entreat you, Sir, as a neighbour, that, should you wish to run mad, you will give warning that I may warn my daughter and servants, but, to be short, recommend, if such be your design, that you will remove to some other place where decent Christian people may not be so readily encountered.

I send no compliments to you, Sir, and am, with injury, a poor digestion and in righteous indignation,
Samuel Wagstaff.

'Hoo!' shouted Bagshaw, and almost handed the letter to Fanny for her perusal. He then did what he seldom did, he laughed; and so passed to his other letter. This one was from his friend 'Vesuvius', who was coming to Lichfield at the invitation of Sim and intended to call to introduce himself. Bagshaw smiled at the letter's loquacious charm. 'Vesuvius' was the most excellent fellow. His interests were hugely diverse, and in the fabric of his proper subject might weave all manner of observations and secondary questions. Bagshaw was amazed at some description, provided by the letter, of presents the writer had made of ribbons, lace and other frivolous things, even alcoholic drink, to the poor about his estate. 'Small comforts', as his correspondent called them, 'and I think of one poor creature, who has these twenty years borne thirteen children and lost eight, who, by my gift, has new ribbons for the hat she wears to church, which like as much keep the thing together, yet have they brought her such joy; and I think of a light which comes in the eyes of old men, more than eighty years old, who have these many years seen all before, yet cannot forbear but show their pleasure at gifts of snuff and cheap twists of tobacco. And therefore we should be mindful, I think, of heart as well as soul, for we do not live unless we know it and should we not know it by more than drill or plough, or by the cold hand of Necessity?'

The firelight was warm as Bagshaw draped his legs across the hearth. He began to think of his own giving and to turn in his mind the softer philosophy of his friend. It saddened him, as the letter dropped from his hand, that he was a straight-laced

115

dog. He had some intimation of how Miss Wagstaff must see him. He might well understand.

A postscript to the letter gave a reminder of the intended visit. Bagshaw wanted really to be gone, but this acquaintance was one to uplift him and soften him, and lend flexibility to principle and indulgence to good.

In the dark the warmth of the fire gradually lulled Fanny, and Bagshaw watched, fondly, as her eyes grew heavier, the orange light lapping at her until it divided her face along her nose. Bagshaw blessed her for her company, which he could not possibly do without, but, this said, roused her and, running a hand down her cheek, dispatched her to bed.

He had intended to read once Fanny left him, but instead went to bed. On the stairs he stopped where the landing gave a view of the city, now winking just beyond his reach. In the night a slanting light was plying the pool, casting a glittering sheen upon it. Some voices – perhaps of children – rang suddenly across it, although he could not see them, and over it, in the corner of the Close, a light burned in the Wagstaffs' house. Bagshaw stared at it, wondering who burned it, but this would not do. He looked forward to the arrival of his friend and determined to build his life again, if only in good works. Turning from the window he continued up the stairs, the key turned in his door and Bagshaw gave himself up to the dark.

Chapter 23

Taplin, Harewood's spy, was very good; hardly a single walk between Sim and Miss Wagstaff escaped his notice. The money that this brought him was welcome, but he enjoyed spying. He loved hurting Harewood, for one thing. It gave him power over the doctor; over both doctors, in fact.

Harewood did not notice this malice. Instead he saw malice in Sim and imputed wickedness to whatever Sim did. He drew up an account of all these wrongs, but among them one thing outweighed the others: worse than everything else was Sim's attempt to steal Miss Wagstaff from him.

It was clear to Harewood that he had to take action. He could not stand by and do nothing. So it was that he dressed carefully that day. This day was to be *the* day: the day he would make his proposal of marriage. He had dressed and re-dressed in readying himself, but settled on his best wig, pristine stockings and an embroidered coat. These were the best that he had.

His walking had improved of late but he was forced to use his carriage to visit Miss Wagstaff. It was tantalising. He left with the carriage blinds down; when he raised them he was there. Likewise he revelled in standing outside her door; and, once admitted, laughed that his heart was racing. Rather farcically, he diagnosed that he was in a state of nervous excitement – he said this aloud – and carefully noted acceleration in his breathing. To these symptoms he might also have added something else: hysteria. He laughed because he wanted to run; he had not felt such a thing since boyhood!

Although like a dog in the traps Harewood had to wait because Miss Wagstaff was busy. She spoke to a servant in another room; he could hear her. It was easy for him to picture her running his home. He might have continued to listen, but the servant came to call him. With a tug at his waistcoat he stood and entered.

Harewood kept the form of his proposal in mind, but forgot it once he was admitted. Miss Wagstaff smiled, extended a hand and he was undone. In this moment she made several impressions upon him. What these were he might not have said. He felt them. It was a mix of all the things that made her essential self. The nearness of her intoxicated him. It was always the same, but today he felt heady. In truth, he nearly forgot himself; he almost put a hand to her face. But then he noticed the contraption upon which she had been working. Miss Wagstaff laughed.

'Oh, I see that you notice the talking machine, Doctor Harewood. It is a contraption of Doctor Sim's.' As she said this she reproached herself.

'What is the thing, Madam?'

Jenny blamed herself for being tactless. It was better not to mention Sim to Harewood; equally it was better not to mention Harewood to Sim. The doctor evinced a gruff interest, if only that he might denounce the device, and she warmed to the task of explaining it.

'You see, Doctor, the box is of wood, which corresponds to the throat and is equipped with a mouth of leather. Air enters the machine here, by a bellows, and may be regulated by a valve, while within the box is a ribbon, stretched between two points, and this, given the passage of air across it and the resonance of the sound within the box, produces a noise that replicates speech, this being subject to alteration by the movement of the lips. I am helping the doctor perfect the machine. It has already attracted much notice.'

Miss Wagstaff spoke with an interest that he had not seen before and he was furious that she had been seduced by Sim into his quackery. Why her father allowed it he could not imagine. If the truth be told he was a little interested, but could not admit of this. He would rather have attempted to swallow the thing whole.

'You are too readily impressed by that gentleman, Miss Wagstaff.'

'I am impressed by myself, Doctor Harewood,' she replied, looking up from the machine, her face quite different. She did not mean to be gracious in saying this. 'I have discovered ingenuity within myself that I did not know I possessed, and I think the better of myself because of it.'

'Your inclination, however, is to think well of the doctor. It is monstrous that my own good works and attention to duty are disregarded as they are.' She looked at him, somewhat askance. 'Miss Wagstaff, allow me to state my case for your consideration. I have, since we spoke on this subject, treated several of the townspeople at most reasonable rates, indeed almost at a loss. You see, I am not such a bad fellow. I have also accomplished a most important development. I have developed a method, Madam, for treating chronic leg ulcers. Is this not worthy of your admiration?'

Miss Wagstaff considered this, and how best she might answer without giving offence. Some innate stubbornness also resisted him. She was aware of his intention to impress her. 'I welcome the attention that you have given to the townspeople, Doctor Harewood. You are very good. I am afraid, as I am not a doctor, that I cannot comprehend your achievement in your new method, but I am sure that it is of the greatest importance.'

She took a chair and bade him do the same. He sat down, but then got up again. Harewood was irritated by her glib answer. In the same way her posture chafed him. She sat with her back straight, her chin up, her hands joined in her lap. He felt that she had no ease with him, that he was a guest for whom she had manners but no warmth.

'Perhaps I distract you from your real interest, Miss Wagstaff? I should be sorry to come between you and Sim's work.'

She gave him a look and sat back. Once she had done this she looked away, and Harewood dropped onto a chair. His head lolled, he flopped out his legs and he let out a long expiration of air, not bothering to hide his vexation. Oh dear; but by degrees he began to consider the matter. The question was, should he proceed? Catching his eye she looked away but not without some humour. She was ready to talk again, if he would give way first. Harewood laughed, and as she looked at him felt strongly her capacity to love – and wanted much that she should love him. He was now impatient with the distance of manners. He wanted to know her in love, to feel her back against his in bed, to come home to her, and so, with a desperate courage, he decided to go on.

'Miss Wagstaff,' he said, earnestly. He used a voice that he reserved for occasions like this. It was the voice that he had used when he proposed to his first wife; and she had accepted him. It was also the one he used at the bed of those who were slipping from him into eternity.

'Forgive me, Doctor Harewood,' she said suddenly. She coloured and became animated. 'We have been friends so long, and it was very rude of me not to enquire further after your work regarding leg ulcers. Please do tell me of it.'

'Miss Wagstaff,' said Harewood with a settled purpose. He would not be deflected and she sat back and composed herself. Harewood managed to get onto one knee. He did this with such difficulty that she almost begged him to desist. Finally, at great length, he arranged himself and she looked at him, smiling, as she waited in a way that was somewhat sad, had he noticed it, but infinitely patient.

'My dear, dear Miss Wagstaff. I have come here not to bicker with you or talk about Doctor Sim. You may guess what I am about to say. My attention to you has been so marked, my hopes for our future life so earnest that you could not mistake my intention or my sincerity. Allow me, Miss Wagstaff, to tell you how ardently I love you and how my whole prospect of future happiness seems to hinge upon this moment and so I hope that you will not disappoint me. Please, my dear Miss Wagstaff, I beg of you, will you consent to be my wife?'

She listened, bending over him as he looked up at her, a spaniel. This image was strong in her mind, and in other circumstances she might have laughed or even run a hand through his hair; such was her affection for him then. She could not but be moved, and she saw something in him that was unknown to the many; that he was a loving man. She was touched that he loved her, although a little embarrassed as it was not reciprocated. She had not always thought well of the doctor, sometimes more, sometimes less, but now she felt a deep gratitude and kindness towards him, more than she had ever done; but she could not marry him.

'My dear Sir, dear Doctor Harewood, I cannot. Please forgive me, Sir, I am sorry.'

Harewood touched her in his reaction; he was like a boy who tried not to cry. She tried to compose her feelings, like a woman schooled in restraint, but felt that she might cry too and hoped beyond anything that the doctor would not. Somewhat rudely he struggled to get up, which he did much more quickly that he had got down, although it hurt him.

'It is Sim who lies behind this, Sim! You will not accept me because you have been blinded by that man. After all, why should my good works, my service, duty, long practice, all my medical researches count for anything in comparison with that mountebank, and toys such as that!' Harewood grew so upset that he had difficulty with his speech. He had a mechanical quality and might have been drawn by strings, jerking and rocking as he spoke.

Miss Wagstaff forced herself to look at him.

'I shall prove to you my worth, Madam. I shall show you who deserves notice and advancement. You will see me in a different light yet, Madam. You will see, you will see!' The doctor, in an awkward motion, attempted something of a bow but almost toppled over. This farce was made greater by his rolling, stumpy walk. He caught her eyes a moment, none the less, as he sought to leave with a modicum of decency. Thereafter he limped from the room, like a pirate in a children's story, swinging one leg. She watched him go. The door banged behind him, the outer door did the same, and she watched him until at last he was gone.

121

Chapter 24

Turning for a moment the wagoner spoke to calm his horses. At his back were two good horses, better fed than he, and he spoke to them kindly.

'Us'll get yer baggage there, Sir, quick enough.'

Bagshaw nodded, but excused himself and moved off. He was thoughtful and pondered the cart, which was drawn under the frontage of the house. He had concerns about the cart, although he moved not because of this but because he had been obliged to shift. He stood in the smell of the man. None the less he would not humiliate him, and suffered it whenever they were close. He knew something of the man and wanted to give him the work if possible.

Again without embarrassing him, Bagshaw glanced at the man. The cartman must have been about half his weight; a man of cheek bones and undershot jaw; a man made of string and without the substance for work, except for his spirit, that is. Otherwise he had a pigtail, a battered hat, which he held at his waist, two red-rimmed eyes and a great anxiety to secure this job; but Bagshaw was uncertain of his cart.

It was a long cart, however, on two reasonable axles, and would probably do. Indeed, since Bagshaw had decided to leave Lichfield he might have considered it had it been worse. What mattered to him was that he got away. He wanted to return home and begin again, although in seclusion; hence he was anxious to remove his property and have done.

He pondered a moment more with regard to the cart, prudently thinking of the security of his goods, which were mostly books, valuable to him and not easily replaced. His long face contracted and he rubbed his hands as, meanwhile, the wagoner shuffled and waited.

Suddenly Bagshaw had had enough of thinking. As the uncertainty vanished from his eyes the cartman gave himself up to his fate. His being offered twice what he had asked was, therefore, hardly to be believed. There was something amiss about this.

'I ain't stealin' no bodies!' he said, and Bagshaw laughed and turned to the house.

Behind them the ruddy bricks climbed and the white dressing about the windows shone brilliantly white. It was a lovely day, and sunlight flooded through the trees. Mindful of this, Bagshaw looked for something that he enjoyed. Over the road the church was a comforting orange brown; the cottage in the grounds let up chimney smoke; and else the city was bright, busy in goings on. It was a good day.

Fanny suddenly appeared in the doorway and watched him; but artful as she was, she seemed to be innocent. She saw that he was almost restored; the pallor of the last week was gone and his cheeks had fleshed out. The ravaged handsomeness had left him, but in place was a bonny – or near bonny – strength and renewal.

She was glad of this but had noticed none the less, on the previous night, how long he had looked into the flames. Such pondering of the coal light pertained, she thought, to a part of him that she did not know. This saddened her because she wanted him to be happy, but none the less they had a bond. She had, she was convinced, grown much in the few months with him. She was acceptable to him, and more, much more than that. This was a wonderful thing. The most marvellous vista had opened for Fanny: her life was full of promise; and, at present, she was terribly excited, looking forward to seeing Bagshaw's estate – a place unknown to her but soon to be her home.

Bagshaw, in entering, chided the girl, although but half seriously. She blocked his way but, civilly, he passed her, she drifted away and the door was shut behind him.

In the absence of their wagoner, whom Bagshaw had dispatched to clean the inside of the cart, there was a to-ing and

fro-ing, up and down stairs. Various things were removed –
mostly books – and Fanny and Bagshaw made repeated journeys.
Once Bagshaw stood and commented upon Fanny's clumping
shoes. This last day he had permitted her to wear her Sunday
frock, and others such were promised her; together, indeed, with
ribbons! Perhaps Bagshaw had some thought of replacing her
strapping boots? As the injunction had passed against ribbons her
hair was bound behind her, which suited the turn of her face.
Her eyes, too, seemed the bolder for it. However, she must guard
against vanity, else the austere regime descended again. Therefore
she was only mildly exultant – indeed lukewarm – in prospect of
losing her boots. She quite said as much, and Bagshaw laughed.

Once more in the hall they put down their last
consignment, and had some thought of fetching another when,
suddenly, the bell sounded at the door. Bagshaw thought it soon
for the wagoner to be back but was glad of it, although he cast a
concerned glance at Fanny. While he encouraged industry he did
not wish her to carry too many heavy books, which she would
persist in, without particular edict to desist. He swung open the
door and in front of him, to his complete surprise, was a woman,
a woman of quality obviously, but such a one as he had seldom
before met.

The woman wore a dress that was entirely plain. It was
extraordinarily so but, this said, it also flattered her. Her hair was
likewise simple. It was very clean, of a warm chestnut, and was
tied and hung in a knot across one shoulder, fastened by a
ribbon. Furthermore she had an artless smile, though engaging,
which plied them in a happy and knowing combination of her
upturned mouth and two fine eyes. She was a vision.

'The doctor has been called away, but I decided to call
without him. I am a day late; I do apologise, Mr Bagshaw.
Fanny!'

The woman was polite to Bagshaw, but turning to
Fanny was warm, recognising her with a full and rich delight.
She knew them!

'Madam,' said Bagshaw inanely. Fanny curtsied. When this was
done they continued to stare at her. The woman smiled, thoughtful.
Her eyes were lit with intelligence, amused at their surprise and
delighted at their awkwardness – especially the rudeness of Bagshaw,
who kept her on the doorstep and gawped at her.

'My name, Mr Bagshaw, is Mary Selvey. You know me, Sir, as "Vesuvius".'

Still Bagshaw would not believe that any connection existed between them.

'You, Madam, are a woman,' he said.

Miss Mary Selvey enjoyed this and Fanny, too, made one of her musical little chuckles. 'Vesuvius' laughed. She did this in a kind way, though; her mouth turned up at the corners and her shoulders shook.

At last Bagshaw recovered. He stood aside, and on rock-steady legs swung downwards into a bow. 'Madam!'

By means of extending an arm Bagshaw indicated the house, but the woman would not come in. She remained on the doorstep and perused him. It was remarkable, in these moments, how her charming eyes and warmth, which had seemed fixed, became clouded. 'Too many are the nincompoop creatures who make such salutations, Mr Bagshaw. Such is not your way, I think, and therefore let us despatch with them.'

Some sense of irony for a moment flooded the whole of Bagshaw's face. His fine eyes twinkled with it and he laughed. 'Certainly, Madam,' he said, and, rising to his full, considerable height, asserted his more usual self for the first time in their exchange. Thus the two, entirely unembarrassed, studied each other. Finally, however, Bagshaw indicated the road. 'I am lately restored, Madam, from illness and a want of spirits. Would you walk with me? I should like to take the air.'

'Out into the many-coloured day!' laughed Fanny, repeating the phrase that recently had often been on Bagshaw's lips; and the woman, who excused herself with great courtesy from Fanny, moved off into the yard. Bagshaw followed her.

'We shall soon return, Fanny,' said Bagshaw, catching her eyes as he crossed over the step, 'We shall not forget you.' Joining the woman – he a foot taller – they walked toward the road, he bowling, she sauntering, and each having to make some allowance for the other, until, reaching the road and the church among the trees, they turned left and passed from sight.

Chapter 25

The unhappiness that Harewood left behind him took some while in clearing. Miss Wagstaff was dispirited, and only the sense that she had done right consoled her; but she had acted properly, and what alternative might there have been?

She felt it necessary to tell her father what she had done, although she had no choice in this. Hardly had he entered the room before he gauged her mood and took up her hand. He was terribly concerned and his tiny eyes were avid, but he relaxed once he found out what affected her; something that gave her a different perspective. She knew that he and Harewood were friends and that he would have welcomed an engagement between them. She knew, too, his strength of character when something fixed in his mind, so it was a relief that he thought more of her wants and desires than his own.

It moved Miss Wagstaff in sitting with her father; indeed it amused her that he trod so carefully. The old man was not always so tactful. For example, when someone told him that they were to dine with the bishop he had said, 'I cannot think why; he does not like you'; while on another occasion, after taxing the bishop on some point of theology, he turned to Jenny and declared, 'He knows nothing about it!' Kind as he was, his speech often preceded consideration. She was glad, therefore, that he was careful not to upset her but talked in terms of his own life; he remembered women he had admired and others who had admired him, recalling how his life might have taken other turns. Finally he said how glad he was to have married as his heart directed him, and then he kissed her, something he seldom did. For a moment he ran one hand down her face and then began to talk in cheerful terms of Sim's talking machine and what a splendid fellow Sim was. Thereafter they spent the remainder of the afternoon together, experimenting further with the machine.

Miss Wagstaff kept to herself over the next day or so, but her work on Sim's machine kept her busy. She had hoped that Sim would call, as she was eager to discuss her experiments, but he did not. It seemed that he was busy, and though she sometimes stood in an upstairs room and looked out into the Close he did not come, nor anyone else.

It suited her well to remain at home, but increasingly she felt unsettled and went out to walk off some of the energy that had gathered in her. There were many walks that she might have: Lichfield was a city in the country and one did not have to walk far to leave it behind. Today she decided to go further afield. After making one or two calls she left the city and took the road that climbed toward Wall. Somewhere near the top she turned and looked around. After this point the city was hidden, which discouraged her from walking any further. From here she might survey the city, and so she stopped to view it. Without intention she immediately noticed the cathedral. It sat crowded by houses, but this was deceiving: there was space about it, and Minster Pool along one side. Behind the cathedral was Stowe Pool and behind that the tower of St Chad's Church. There were other spires too, and between them all the houses rubbed shoulders, looking as though there was scarcely a gap between them. She gazed, narrowing her fine eyes, and traced fingers of chimney smoke, or light catching here and there, and then took a great draught of country air and folded her arms.

She became absorbed in looking and, for this reason, did not appreciate that a horseman had for a moment or so been making a steady progress toward her. Indeed, not until he spoke did she even realise that he was there, but the voice she immediately knew; although, none the less, she still jumped and coloured.

'Miss Wagstaff, good afternoon, what a pleasure to meet you here.'

Sim smiled from the back of his brown, fine mare, towering over her, given his own size and lofty station. The horse turned its great head toward her and Sim let the reins go slack, shifting so that his weight moved forward onto his big red hands on the pommel. He had been to a patient in Wall, and behind him was a box that carried all the impedimenta of his working day. His colour was up as he smiled down at her, and his eyes were large and white. 'You are not tired? You have not walked too far?'

She grew red and shook her head.

'No, Sir.'

There came a moment when each of them inspected, as it seemed, the other. For her, Sim, perched atop his mare, looked enormous, while he studied her with that look of his which seemed to penetrate, a kind expression but searching and perhaps rude, given its unrelenting extent. Nonetheless, she did not appear to mind it and raised one hand to brush a wisp of dark hair from her face, her green eyes narrowed against the light, so that the sun in them seemed to pick out flecks of brown around the black of the iris. She did not look away, and her cheeks were puckered with a trace of a smile.

'I have been most industrious,' she said, after a moment. 'I have carried out all the experiments that you required of me upon the talking machine and have made tremendous progress.'

Miss Wagstaff said this with so great an eagerness to please, and such enthusiasm for the machine, that Sim was delighted and laughed. 'Excellent! Thank you, thank you. You see how busy I am. What might I do without you?'

She smiled and looked pleased, and he grinned and shifted to look into her face as she turned away a moment, in this seeking out her fine eyes, enjoying, as he did, the green of them but most pertinently their combination with the black eyebrows over them, which angled so sharply toward her nose and then widened and imperceptibly ended at their other corners.

'I have news for you,' he said, 'about our talking machine.' She lifted her face and looked, interested. 'I have received a challenge from a gentleman with whom I have lately been corresponding. He is owner of a manufactory; an engineer, a gentleman and a scientist. He has promised me a thousand pounds if I can make our machine recite an agreed text. A thousand pounds! Think of the good that could be done with that!'

'Why, you might support the education of a number of children,' she replied, growing warm, her voice quickening, 'or publish and make widely known our treatise on female education, or relieve much poverty among the old and infirm.'

'All manner of things,' said Sim, 'and all of them good; but I shall need your help. Do I ask too much of you, Miss Wagstaff?'

'No, indeed not!' she said, coming right up alongside the neck of the horse, so that her face came somewhere up to the level of his right thigh, in such a relation to him that he might almost have reached down and run a hand through her hair, which was so rich with its rimed black brown. He might cheerfully have done it too. Once more the two looked at each other.

'Is not Doctor Harewood a rascal?' said Sim suddenly.

'What do you mean, Sir?'

Miss Wagstaff looked confused and Sim was not slow to notice that she blushed and was not altogether comfortable. This was something he did not understand or like. He wondered after the cause of this and a moment of some anxiety rose up in him, but he contained it and gave nothing away, except that his kindly, fine eyes once more applied themselves to her and sought to define her feelings, although in his warm, incidental, inconspicuous way.

'Have you not heard, Miss Wagstaff, that he intends to perform an operation upon a poor soul from the town, a transfusion, if you please, publicly, as if his practice were some sort of pleasure garden attraction? A transfusion! Such a thing may not be done without risk and yet he is prepared to accept this, not so much, in my view, for the good of the patient concerned, but to aggrandise himself in the public estimation and at my expense. How dare he trifle with the life of a patient! It is intolerable!'

Sim was, in saying this, quite another man from the one whom Miss Wagstaff had hitherto seen. He stiffened visibly in his saddle and his ploughboy face, with the apples in his cheeks, became a more general red. The sudden annoyance was also very plain in his eyes. He was disagreeable, and Miss Wagstaff was a trifle embarrassed and cast round for some diversion, which Sim saw; something that seemed to irritate him further. For a moment she thought that he was about to take rein and ride off.

'I am sorry if this displeases you,' he said, shortly. His eyes fell heavily upon her and he drew his mouth into a straight line. Clearly he had little more to add, and she could sense that he was about to go. Such was her confusion, however, at this sudden turn that she could not submit to this. She looked up at him and put a hand on one rein.

'No, Sir, why should it?'

'You are not?'

'No, Sir. If what you tell me is true then I am shocked but I am not displeased, Sir, at least for my sake.'

Sim seemed to digest this information and took a remarkable amount of time in doing so; at least it appeared so to her. She waited for him as he turned it over behind his eyes, becoming once again, as she watched him, more relaxed and sunny by degrees, so that, at length, he became himself again. He looked down at her and smiled.

'I am so sorry,' he said. 'You must be tired; do please take my place. I can walk. It will be good for me, and poor old Doctor' – Sim called his horse by this name – 'will be glad to have you on her back instead of my great weight.'

It was more usual for ladies to ride side-saddle at this time; the expectation was that a woman of quality would ride side-on, although riding astride was not unknown. This may have explained a moment of uncertainty on the part of Miss Wagstaff, but Sim waved this away, perceiving the nature of her reluctance.

Perhaps he rather made some play of his athleticism, but that moment saw him rise in the saddle, and the next second after, swinging one leg over and round, he had dropped onto the ground beside her, close to her, so close that she might now smell him. This was not, may it be said, the foul smell of dirty linen but a fresh, honest, working man smell, a man of industry and also flesh and blood. The two stood so near to one another that she felt something of the heat of him. Miss Wagstaff was for a moment embarrassed but then raised her head and from close by looked into his face, without reserve or thought of anything else, and so when the doctor put a big hand on each of her shoulders it seemed right that he did so. She dropped her head a moment and smiled and turned, so that her cheek brushed his hand on one side, and then played her green eyes over him, noting every line and every flaw, though all seemed beautiful to her, and then she turned her mouth to his, for the first time in her life as a woman, and kissed him.

The moment seemed to envelop them both, so that after it was done they both seemed shocked by it. Indeed it was Miss Wagstaff who collected herself before the doctor, who now endeared himself to her by seeming so embarrassed. She smiled and put one hand briefly to his face. In doing this she collected and held his eyes, and he was transfixed. He had long thought that she had the most beautiful eyes of anyone of his acquaintance, but now they smiled for him, something that produced in him an intense sense of humility and gratitude, as well as wonder that so much goodness and affection could convey itself by them. For one moment more they embraced.

'Nay, Sir,' she laughed as he enveloped her in his great arms and quite squeezed the life from her. He was an awkward lover, this doctor of hers, but she realised now something that was precious to her, and rich and good, and full of the most wonderful promise; that she loved him and he her.

When a moment or so more passed them by they decided that they could not stand there indefinitely, although this spot seemed world enough; but sensibly, and since the doctor needed to return home, they walked back down the hill towards the city. She would not ride, not being dressed for it, but instead, one on either side of the horse's head and each of them seemingly leading it, they strolled back to Lichfield, for as long as they dared holding hands under the bridle.

Chapter 26

Doctor Harewood had been going home when the weight of his melancholy seemed to tire his horse, and his slow progress came to a halt in the region of Stowe Pool. The society of his housekeeper did not draw him on and so, wanting to be private, he led his horse off the road to the water.

He was at peace in the dark and might have stood there longer, but his horse disturbed him. The moment was broken and, idly, he ran a hand down his face and looked about him. Nearby were the church, some cottages and Mr Bagshaw's former house. These things were drawn in black ink, something he might have enjoyed, but he was dead to it. In the same way he could not enjoy the light on the water. There was moonlight on the pool and beyond this the city raised its irregular shape, displaying lights here and there. If he followed them he came to the cathedral, and at the base of this were the lit windows of the house where Miss Wagstaff lived – and where she had refused him.

Poor Harewood had that day received a report from Taplin, news that had shocked him. The news was something he had half known; that Sim and Miss Wagstaff were familiar, and some intimacy was suspected between them. Thus she, it seemed, his own dear Miss Wagstaff had been overset by that young man, as so many were, except him. She, who had refused him, had given herself to Sim; it was too much to bear.

Away, across the water, he could see her home, and in one of the squares of orange she probably sat and read and passed the night by, she within and he without, utterly without.

At last he decided to leave, but stood a moment. He was bitterly disappointed but wanted to mark, in a moment of reflection, that he loved Jenny Wagstaff; let it be said one last time. Indeed he thought so kindly of her that the water rose in his eyes, but this affection was spoiled, and even as he thought of her a great annoyance was at work in him. He struck his hat against his leg and forced it onto his head.

That day Harewood had arranged to use the Guild Hall so that an audience might watch him at work. His intention was to perform a sensational operation: with one stroke he would exalt his reputation. All was now in train to bring this about, and he had no doubt that it would damage Sim.

Much to his satisfaction the city was already talking of his wonder. It was to be a transfusion; a transfusion of blood from one person to another. Never in the history of Lichfield had such a thing been done or, he believed, in the entire world. There was some risk in it, but he had selected a patient who had most to gain. However, he expected to vindicate himself, especially so before Miss Wagstaff, his dear Miss Wagstaff who was so deluded, and Sim, whose name he could but with difficulty even so much as mention.

Chapter 27

Sim was vexed by the plan for the transfusion. In many ways it was like a case of the itch. Although he wanted to ignore it he could not do so. For one thing it interested him, but it also appalled him. His rivalry with Harewood had now become manic, and it seemed to Sim that Harewood had become unhinged. Harewood was now prepared to risk a patient's life. Matters had run out of hand, and Sim wished to bring the enmity between them to an end.

He had not spoken to Harewood since their argument after Harewood's accident. Sim suspected that he would remember this but decided to approach him. So it was that he waited by the western front of the cathedral. Harewood walked by Stowe Pool in the evening and sometimes returned through the Close. Of course, Harewood might not be polite, but he would ignore this and press to the heart of the matter. The neutral ground of the Close would, he hoped, make Harewood more amenable, and in the shadow of the cathedral too, surely Harewood, Anglican as he was, would be more receptive to what he had to say.

It seemed natural that Sim should find himself in that quarter and he walked up to the front. In this place the cathedral was like a cliff face, possessed of a bulk that intruded upon one's notice. It had a sort of personality, which was something Sim found fascinating. To stand in its presence was an oddly personal thing, and he felt a strange sense of concord with the fabric of it.

He rocked on his heels as he looked at the building, with his hands behind his back, comfortable and at peace. As his mind wandered he thought of his water closet, his talking machine, a new weathervane, a device to duplicate writing and other things beside, all in short order; but his mind returned to the cathedral. As was his custom he looked up at it. Overhead the gable spanned the two frontal towers. Each tower supported a spire, and each was topped in gold. All was so pleasing.

In this there was something else that he enjoyed above all. Sim loved the swifts that soared around the tops of the spires. He grew almost gay as he watched them and tried to follow them against the light. For a moment he would fix one in his sight, then the bird would flit aside; a second would catch his eye, and then this would become confused with another.

So great was the pleasure that he found in this that he decided Miss Wagstaff must share it with him. He forgot about Harewood and set off to her home beyond the cathedral. Miss Wagstaff was at leisure when the knock sounded at the door. She was reading but listened, as she suspected that the summons was for her. That day she had been out and walked back with Sim, so had no expectation of it being him, but when she heard his voice she jumped up – and so found herself on the path to the birds.

When they arrived outside the Front the birds were still in full play, but Sim spent a moment in watching her. He did this unashamedly. Rogue as he was, he did it partly to flatter her, partly to tease and partly because she was so lovely. Miss Wagstaff wore a white dress, with flowers of yellow embroidered on it and an apron over it. The exercise had brought up her colour and this made her eyes bright; and he smiled as she, without design, put down her chin and looked at him, smiling the smile that he had learned to prize, her dark brows black over her eyes.

It was not strictly proper, or wise for that matter, but Sim of a sudden gave her shoulders a little shake. 'You will go to a ball, my lady.'

The George sometimes hosted balls and Sim, in this moment, wanted much to dance with Jenny. He was full of this: he would have enjoyed it, but something more. He wanted to exchange her in the dance for another partner, only to find her again. He pictured them, just on the point of passing behind their line. Almost in motion Sim took her hands, and they could almost hear the music and feel the dance. A laugh, and he grew slack and quite easy. He released her, but just before he did so he pulled her close. This was an intimacy that was not wise or proper and she pulled away, but briefly they were joined. For a moment he looked into the greeny brown of her eyes, with all the wonder of her essential self in them. He let her go and they fell in, like soldiers, adopting a more decorous relationship, but Sim still stood and looked at her, now entirely sincere, prizing her, glad and grateful for this liaison that grew ever more consuming for him.

He might have stood like this for some time in his admiration of Miss Wagstaff, but he became aware, somewhat slowly, that she had become uncomfortable. Indeed she was a little embarrassed. It had not been wise that she had behaved as she had in a public place. This was a source of regret to her, but was not the whole of her concern. Sim turned round, following her eyes. On the footpath under the trees, some yards to the side, Harewood stood and watched them. Immediately Sim excused himself.

'Forgive me, Jenny; I must speak to the doctor.' Thus she was left to walk herself home, or watch what ensued, as was the case.

Harewood realised that Sim had taken an interest in him. This was unwelcome, and he moved off. In this he demonstrated his disgust at seeing their intimacy, which he implied by stomping away, swinging a leg, his nose in the air, one hand upon a hip. It was meant to be very damning; in fact it was a spectacle. None the less he stamped off. In his attempt to escape he managed to hobble away quite quickly. He headed for the gap in the Close that led on to Beacon Street. This was only fifty yards or so from him, but he must move to his left to reach it; Sim might be more direct.

'Doctor Harewood!'

The doctor stopped, although he considered ignoring the appeal. While his back was turned his mind raced: what manner should he adopt? His first thought was to be cautious. Despite this, almost as soon as he turned, he betrayed his dislike. Harewood sometimes called Sim the 'ploughboy': his 'vulgar' walk was the cause of this. As Sim bowled up Harewood despised him for it, which Sim saw, but refused to be distracted by it.

'Forgive me, Doctor Harewood,' said Sim, 'but I must beg a moment of your time.'

Harewood said something about not being at work. He idly asked if Sim were unwell, implying that Sim could not treat himself. As before, Sim ignored the attempt to affront him.

'I understand, Sir, that you are soon to transfer blood from one person to another in a public operation in the Guildhall?'

'If you wish for a ticket,' said Harewood, 'you must purchase one for yourself. You may be admitted to the rear of the hall. I would not wish your patients to lose the benefit of my instruction.'

'No, Sir. I do not wish to attend. Sir, you hold an eminent place in this community and have served it well for several years. Many are the people who owe their wellbeing to you, indeed their very lives. Surely, Sir, because of a spirit of competition that may have arisen between us, there is no need for you to hazard your reputation in this manner?'

'My reputation, Sir? Of what concern is that to you?'

It was vexing that a defensive note had crept into their conversation. Sim dropped his head and glanced at Harewood. He wished that they might speak plainly. Consequently he decided to be more direct. He would be frank, in the hope that Harewood would respect his candour.

'I beg your pardon, Sir, I prevaricate. Allow me to be blunt. I am concerned that I, by attracting some of your former patients to me, have induced you to undertake this dangerous experiment. Surely you are mistaken, Sir? Recollect yourself and do not proceed with this undertaking. Do not risk the life of your patient by such an expedient.'

At once Sim knew that he had made the matter worse. Harewood stared at him and Sim watched in resignation. Harewood gulped, his Adam's apple bunched and fell, and Sim waited.

'You think well of yourself,' said Harewood, 'that you say this to me. Are you so conceited as to think that I might pay you the least regard?'

Sim felt the lick of irritation and he noticed, in a moment of clarity, how his throat contracted. As a consequence of this his breathing grew reedy and laboured. This thought served to distract him, and consequently he managed to keep his temper. He even began to say something conciliatory, sticking to his purpose doggedly, but Harewood interrupted and reiterated his complete disregard of him.

'Then why, Sir,' said Sim, growing warm, 'have you been so busy with your pen? Do you deny, upon your honour, that you wrote the poem about me that appeared in the *Gentleman's Magazine*?' Sim had felt the tug of annoyance on his arm again and now let the dog slip.

Harewood ignored his question. 'And you, Sir, do you deny that you are an atheist? More than this, if that were not monstrous enough, are you not also a base fraud to misrepresent your trifles to Mr Wagstaff, knowing that he ascribes an entirely different significance to them? I am bound to ask if Miss Wagstaff knows the extent of your duplicity?'

'Do not mention that lady,' said Sim. 'She is no concern of yours.'

'Indeed,' snapped Harewood. 'Would that I might say as much for you! You know very well, Sir, the expectations that I had in that quarter and how disappointed I have been.'

Sim measured Harewood for a blow. He wanted to plant his bunched fist upon the side of Harewood's jaw. The thought of this was pleasing and he let Harewood see the possibility of it, but restrained himself.

'Now, Sir, we discover your motive,' he said instead. Harewood stood by, sourly. 'To increase your standing at my expense, both as a physician and a man, you are prepared to risk the life of a patient: not through medical necessity, not even for the advancement of knowledge, but through injured pride and bitterness. Such a doctor are you, Mr Harewood.'

One might have thought that Harewood had been slapped; a sort of motion ran through him. Nor was it easy to imagine that he could, short of violence, be angrier, but he collected himself. 'And you,' he said, 'you cannot bear that I should gain precedence over you, that my name might be remembered and yours forgotten; that I, and not you, Doctor, might be the better physician and become known as such; and you talk to me of vanity, Sir.'

'You will not conduct this operation!' said Sim. 'I shall not permit this operation to proceed!' He came quite up to Harewood, the gap between the two men now so short that each was uncomfortably aware of the other. Each could smell the powder of the other, which they used to sweeten their persons in the hot summer weather. Harewood, finding a spirit that surprised him, did not flinch or move at all.

'And I shall not permit you to disrupt me.'

There was a moment when the two stood and glared at each other, until Harewood thought that he should move. His heart was now like a bird beating its wings at a window and he could not say how long his spirit would last. In defiance he gave Sim one last stare, bowed with great politeness to Miss Wagstaff, then turned, carrying on his way, with Sim and Miss Wagstaff watching every step that he took.

Chapter 28

Sim was now determined to prevent the transfusion, and bribed himself passage into the Guildhall on the night of the operation. He also asked Taplin to supply men who might be relied upon. Harewood, unknown to Sim, had also paid him to do the same thing.

All this was most complicated for Taplin, who had such awkward demands made upon him. He was too good in seeking to oblige everyone, but had some idea how he might please everybody.

These preparations were some of many that the doctors made before the event, particularly Harewood. Despite this, laughably, they pretended to be unaffected. In reality, each man thought that the night would end in violence. Even in those moments when they forgot the operation this fear came back to them.

This thought was a black dog that both men came to accept. None the less, when Sim confided this to Jenny she was not sympathetic. She told him, simply, not to interrupt the operation. She also said that if he attended then so would she. He begged her not to go, or bring her father, as would be the case, but she was adamant: if he did not go nor would she; if he did go then she would too.

It may be best to say little of the argument that arose from this; the mutual accusations of stubbornness, and so on. It was a

140

subject that created some friction between them, but come the day Sim hid himself away in the Guildhall. Unknown to Harewood his final preparations were overlooked by Sim, who patiently waited for his time.

When the first of the public made their way into the hall the lights were burning at the far end. Harewood had three tables standing where the natural light was strongest; added to this he had hung supplementary lighting. This was entirely practical, but there was something strange about it. It seemed like a scene of the occult.

When the hall began to fill Harewood had to stop lesser people from taking the seats of their betters. (Rather pointedly, among these people were the connections of his patient.) The doctor placed his own supporters at the front, but this was his privilege.

In two backward rows were men who stank of night soil. (It may not have been night soil; in fairness, it might have been cattle.) Their hard eyes and rough hands may have belied a thirst for knowledge. On the other hand, the presence of Taplin among them suggested that they were his men, who were yet to prove their loyalty for one or the other.

Somewhere at the rear, but unseen by the audience, Harewood watched as the room filled. The doctor objected to the atmosphere that was brewing. In the long room pipe smoke was rising, and so many people talked that the place was like an ale house. There was something too that suggested gaming. Harewood narrowed his eyes at this suspicion. One would not have known that a woman was about to be operated upon.

It seemed odd, but while Harewood despised his audience he would not enter without their notice. In fact, he was obliged to enter more than once. Only on the third occasion did they see him. Now in his element, as the heads turned he walked on, as if he paid no heed to it.

He was followed by a plump woman of middle years. She was to be the beneficiary. Appropriately, perhaps, she wore white, a long robe, which bared her arms. Once people turned from him they looked to her, but she would not look at them and so presented a profile of a hook nose and weak chin with flesh hanging under it. After her walked a man in whom one might see some of her features. This was her brother, Mr Bott.

141

He wore an open shirt and had prepared by rolling up his sleeves. Happily the veins were prominent in his knotted arms. He chanced the many eyes, but not with charity towards the onlookers.

When they reached the front the brother and sister joined hands. In this they looked like the children that they had once been. The audience were quick to notice the feeling between them. This interest in them was something that Harewood seemed to sense and, as if he resented it, he suddenly strode out in front. He adopted his most solemn face and waited for the eyes to settle on him.

'Esteemed patrons, ladies and gentlemen, distinguished colleagues, members of the clergy, good people of Lichfield. I am gratified and honoured, nay, moved, by your attention to me. Indeed, though I come from a respectable family it is by my own merit that I stand before you. One thing, however: I could not be the man that I am but for my patrons. I could not throw back the barriers of learning or do the good for which I am, forgive me, justly praised . . .'

It was necessary for him to remember his patrons, of course, although some may question the duration of this process. In fairness, though, one minute can easily run into two and so into five. So it was with the doctor.

Although this outpouring continued unabated, midway along its course the doctor became distracted. In looking along the backward rows he noticed Jenny. This was like a sleeve catching on a hedge. She made him think of Sim, and in turn he sought out Taplin. Goodness knows, though, what purpose this achieved. Taplin looked at him like a head on a gibbet spike. Harewood went on. 'It is no flattery or complacency that encourages me in the opinion that such an experiment has never before been attempted. Hitherto transfusions of blood have been made only between animals, or from animal to man, but the difficulties attendant upon the procedure have hampered its development. I have solved those problems . . .'

While his patient, Mrs Ayres, stood shivering, Harewood began to explain the wonder that he was about to perform. He did this by describing items or presenting them. Most of what he showed created little impact, but some good came of this; the general incomprehension deflated him. At last he began to better understand what failure might mean. He had understood it in terms of himself, but he realised, finally, the significance to the woman who waited for him. She deserved better than to be taken for granted.

It was strange, but as doubt at last affected Harewood a similar thing discouraged Sim. Sim found that he did not care for his isolation. He did not like to be confined and his joints were now painful, particularly his back. He was frightened, too, that the door, shut to hide him, would be locked from without. To speak the truth he was unsettled, and began to doubt the wisdom of what he did. Was he already too late? He had no idea of what transpired. Beyond a certain point it might be better to let things proceed. Sim was also conscious of the furore that he was about to cause. This was not a happy thought. He pondered the hurt that might be caused to his career. This was such that he began to think of remaining where he was.

At the front the action was already underway, although the point beyond which recall was impossible had not yet occurred. Matters had proceeded to the donor and recipient taking their stations. As the crowd watched Harewood fixed a tourniquet to Mr Bott. The blade shone in the lights and the moment came.

'Oosh!' Mr Bott winced and made a cry. A similar noise repeated through the crowd. Harewood ignored it and inserted into the arm a tapered silver tube. He bent over to do this, pressing his lips as he struggled to fix the flanges (like butterfly wings) that were attached to it. In each of these were two holes, and through each hole was a strand of leather that Harewood cross-threaded, crossed behind the arm and secured in front. With this done he blocked the tube, which had begun to leak blood. The doctor inserted a rod into the tube to do this, and once it was done he could relax. He raised his head, and it was only now that he noticed a commotion in the hall. He had been concentrating so hard that he had not noticed it before. He heard footsteps and sudden noise. Of a sudden there was shouting.

'Stop this experiment, you damned quack!'

Sim, who seemed to have appeared from the floor itself, was striding up the aisle. As he came every head turned up at him. At the back they stood as he passed; at the front they turned around.

'How dare you, Sir!'

143

'My pardon, Mrs Ayres, Mr Bott,' said Sim, brushing Harewood aside, 'but I have been driven to come here.' Taplin, with the others, squabbling between them, made way up the aisle. Sim hastened.

'I would have you know,' said Sim, loudly, 'that Doctor Harewood risks Mrs Ayres's life here because of a jealous rivalry with me. He does not know his business.' Taplin and the others reached him, and jostling commenced around him. Sim raised his voice and the first scuffle took place between him and another, with Taplin seeking, it appeared, to intervene between Sim and this other man.

'Do not permit him to proceed,' shouted Sim, struggling now. 'He takes no care of this woman's life.' He threw off the embrace of a large farm worker, showing great strength, but the man persisted. 'He thinks only of himself!'

He was now being engulfed, with a token number of men in some way seeming to support him. Taplin was among these men, shouting 'Unhand the doctor! Unhand the doctor!' Once, however, when he thought that he might do so without being seen, he punched Sim from the back. 'Unhand the doctor,' he shouted as he pulled his hand away.

It was time for the doctor's true friends to come forward. It happened just as Sim had feared. He knew that it might come to this, and it did. Miss Wagstaff began to make her way toward him.

'Jenny! Jenny! Come here, Ma'am, at once!'

She ignored her father and so he too came forward, although Jenny was already embroiled with the men. The men were mostly more than six feet tall and an average weight of fourteen stone. She was five foot eight and nine stone, and most decidedly feminine. Of course she had no intention to fight. She meant to intervene, calm and shame, to come between Sim and his persecutors, but she was wrong to think that she might bring order to the riot. There was a moment perhaps of surprise, when they realised that a woman was among them, but thereafter the fight went on as before.

At this point her father was knocked over. Jenny cried out, but seeing him back on his legs laid hands again and, as often as she was pushed aside, and under the interference of her father, she kept on and moved among the crush as it blundered to the door. 'Please, please, I beg of you, desist in this. Spare the doctor any further embarrassment.'

This appeal to reason was a vain thing. It was laughable that Jenny believed they might be brought to reason. The men ignored her, as of course they would. Suddenly Sim called her by name. He begged her to retire, but the rather desperate tone of this seemed only to inspire her. 'I say desist!' she shouted, grabbing hold of one dirty creature who still had the muck about him of his trade. The two thereafter had a short contest, although he was gentle enough in his way. Worst were his impertinent hands, but he put her aside – although he did this by putting her in the way of the commotion. There was a moment when she had her back turned to the men and seemed to resist them. For a moment she seemed to stay the weight of them all; then she was knocked flat and the herd trampled her underfoot. Just as he was shoved through the door Sim saw her. In the midst of everything they were joined. The one looked at the other, over the weight and crush, and then he was moved on.

Once Sim was sent on his way; once he had received a last kick; once they had sent him tumbling and he had staggered off, without so much as a look behind him, he sat – safe – and reviewed the last dreadful minutes. His recollections were fragmented, lurid but jumbled. He could see, for instance, Mr Wagstaff with a bloodied nose. The old man looked like a child covered in jam. He could see Jenny, too, fighting for him. It mortified him that she had been trampled, but he reassured himself. Amid the gall and bitter regret that he felt at least he knew she had got to her feet.

The doctor was very much in Jenny's thoughts. As he thought of her so she thought of him; but while she did so she also took stock. The room, which had been like a tavern, was now like a tavern after a brawl. Around her were upturned chairs, with blood on the boards; but worse than this, Mrs Ayres sobbed with an abandoned quality. Jenny intended to comfort her, but first wiped at her father's nose. He was furious, and she had to contend his considerable wrath. In the midst of all this she began to feel unwell, which took her unawares. At one moment she was herself, then felt faint. At length she had to submit to the final indignity of Harewood coming to relieve her.

When she became herself again Jenny wanted to go and enquire after Sim, but someone came forward to put her mind at rest. The men, anyway, had long since retired to the Dolphin Inn. There was no reason for her to remain and she, her father and many others left. Only a rump remained to see Harewood complete the transfusion. It was done, at last. Thereafter they all went home. It only remained to be seen whether Mrs Ayres lived or died.

Chapter 29

On the morning after the transfusion Harewood waited for news. He wanted to publish an account of the operation, if the patient lived. He also wanted to sue Sim but, again, awaited the outcome. The patient's death might serve to vindicate the upstart.

The doctor bent over his papers in a room overlooking the road and failed to see that Miss Wagstaff passed by; but she ignored his house. She blamed him, not Sim, for the previous evening. She went to call on Mrs Ayres out of concern, but partly, too, to blame Harewood and try to exonerate Sim.

In so far as Sim was concerned he had sometimes forgotten the incident. When recollection returned to him he also felt differently about it. The pain of one of his patients, whom he could little help, altered his perspective.

About the time that Sim left this patient Harewood was preparing to leave home. He was late, and the daily round would not wait. Some mornings he had ridden thirty miles by that time. Firstly, however, he would call upon Mrs Ayres, since he could wait not a minute longer. Before he left, having called for his horse, he looked through the window into the road. Harewood wondered at the detachment of the onward going. The outside world went on as it ever did. A woman clung to life and yet nothing changed. The wheels turned, sun shone on the water and geese made noise in the road; all the commonplaces of the everyday.

So great was this sense of the ordinary that Harewood was shocked as he suddenly saw a horse being brought to a stiff-legged halt. He knew, of course, what this meant. He was not surprised to be sent for thus, but he recognised the boy on the horse. A servant moved toward the door but Harewood went himself. The boy was Sam, whose father worked at Edial Hall, where Mrs Ayres worked. There was another clatter at the door and Harewood opened it. The boy was red-faced and breathless. 'Beggin' yer pardon, Master, yume wanted at the 'all. Quick!'

The doctor had known what would be said, but the words shocked him for all that. He lifted a hand as Sam began to repeat himself. The truth was that he did not know what to do, but he must do something and promised to go. The boy was satisfied and sprang like a monkey onto the back of his horse. He kicked it, it jerked into motion, and the great rump and Sam's thin back retreated from the doctor's view.

Harewood was wry as he watched the boy. Sam seemed so proud of the part that he had played in fetching him and he clearly had great confidence in him. Had Sam only known that the doctor was now full of doubt; but at least he thought of his patient and not of himself. Suddenly he called again, loudly, for his horse and determined to do what he could.

The distance between Harewood's home and the hall was perhaps three miles, near enough to reach it quickly; soon enough, he hoped. Five minutes later the doctor clattered out into the road. His horse was a good one, but doctor and horse were hampered by his trunk. This jumped behind him, interfering with their progress. It was a jangling, uncomfortable ride and Harewood was further hampered by Pipe Hill, which lifted the Walsall Road steeply. At last, however, the hill rounded off and Harewood took the road to the right. Here he managed to do a disjointed gallop and, at length, came to the boundary of the hall. Some yards further on he reached the gate and turned into the precinct.

In the yard he threw himself off and struggled with the straps that retained the case on the rear of the saddle. Someone took the horse. Marching to the door he was met on the step by Mrs Ayres. All the bustle and forward motion of the doctor came to a sudden halt.

148

'Oh doctor,' she said, 'I am so much better, bless you, how can I ever thank you, but it's Miss Wagstaff. She's taken ill.'

In this moment his thoughts jostled one on top of another. He was elated to see her; she was clearly improved; but Miss Wagstaff?

'She came to call on me,' said Mrs Ayres. Quickly she took his arm, but he was unsettled. Harewood tried to compose himself but could not bring his mind to bear. For one thing he felt like two men. The doctor, in coat, breeches and wig, was one, but he was more than that. Something of his feelings for her stirred. He was shy, too, embarrassed because of what had happened on the previous night. He strongly suspected that she would not wish him to treat her.

He entered the room behind a pleasantry, but it was as he feared. For this reason he was only mildly hurt when Miss Wagstaff turned away as he approached her.

'Madam,' he said, 'it distresses me to see you in such a condition.'

Ignoring, excusing, her reluctance, Harewood knelt beside her and took up a wrist.

'I am quite well, Doctor,' she said sharply, 'Only a little tired.'

Harewood was attentive to everything she said but ignored her assurance that she was well. By her reluctant leave he questioned her, and she was forced to explain how she felt when she became ill. He listened and, as he did so, took her head in his hands and looked into her eyes, almost as a lover might have done. She consented in this, a little bashful, somewhat prickly, and the doctor was for a moment aware of her as a woman while he did it. He could read much in her eyes and could see that she was unwell. He also saw into himself, and found a draw in their mingled green and brown and in the fine brows over her eyes. He released her, but the tips of his finger ends brushed the turn of her cheekbones for a moment; then he smiled for her as he finally let her go.

'You did well to send for me, Mrs Ayres, but I perceive no immediate danger,' he said, getting to his feet. 'I shall send my carriage, Ma'am,' he turned now to Miss Wagstaff, 'to collect you and transport you home. I shall also write a note to Doctor Sim who, of course, will now have the honour of treating you.'

Thereafter he bowed to the ladies, instructed Mrs Ayres to go to her bed and rushed off, impatient to complete his rounds and begin his legal action against Sim.

Chapter 30

While Miss Wagstaff slept, Sim looked from the window of her bedroom into the garden. Below him was a jangle of colours and some of the taller shrubs almost reached him. He wanted to be outside but, turning once to look at Jenny, dutifully remained where he was.

The room was a simple one. It had a carpet, fireplace and two paintings, together with drawings of Jenny's own. It also had two chairs, a chest, dressing table and the bed.

Sim listened to the rise and fall of Jenny's breathing, concentration in his eyes, but he returned to the window. Over the marsh there was sunlight on Stowe Pool, which he enjoyed. Beyond it was the tower of St Chad's Church and near it some common houses. Near them were also two houses of greater wealth, among greenery. In one of these Mr Bagshaw had lived, with Fanny, and Sim could see the white stone dressing on it.

He glanced again at Jenny and then looked outward once more, his big figure drawn in outline against the light, a silhouette that faithfully recorded him as he had removed his wig. He listened to her breathing, but thought of other things by turns, such as the suit Harewood had brought against him. This was very troublesome, but he also thought of Harewood's success. It irked Sim that Harewood had outdone him. He knew, without vanity, that he was the better physician, and yet found himself relegated by a lesser man.

In the bed Jenny stirred, and he left the window and sat beside her bed. After a moment she looked at him, though firstly through rather befuddled eyes. It took her a moment to recognise him and recall his being there, but she smiled and extended a hand across the covers to him, a white, cold hand at the end of a thin arm.

She had been ill now for a week, perhaps a little less. Since Doctor Harewood's carriage had brought her home from Edial she had not left the house and seldom left her bed.

'You are better today,' said Sim, rubbing her right hand. He smiled and, with a glance at the door, kissed her, then sank back onto his seat, which creaked under him.

'I think that we shall have you well very soon now,' he said. He smiled again and linked his big fingers with hers, but in reality performed a trick. She was unaware that he had done it, so good was he. He distracted her, but at the same time moved his hand down her arm and measured her pulse. Sim, however, was not the only one to dissemble.

'I shall get up today,' Jenny said, brightly. 'I am well enough now.'

It moved him that she tried to deceive him, but she had not. 'No,' he whispered.

'I wish to be out,' she cried, sinking back onto her pillow, and briefly giving way to misery.

He said nothing but rubbed her hand, thinking and wondering how much he was affected to see her ill. It was strange; she had never engaged him so much as now. The sense he had of her, in word and manner and all that made her, distracted him. Toward each patient he felt a bond, but this was now doubled. He intensely felt the care of her but, more than this, she was so beautiful. There was something now in the least thing to engage him; in her hair, for example, even in dishevelment its brown had never seemed so brown or its texture as fine as he turned it between his fingers. He traced the turn of her cheeks against her hair and studied her closely but without embarrassment, half a lover, half a doctor.

Jenny's eyes told him much. Sim could see her illness in them but was encouraged, too, as she looked at him and laughed as she patted his hand. She supported him, and he was moved to see her affection for him. He was humbled by her affection, and

152

he found this acceptance of him as he was more satisfying than the highest qualification that he had or would ever attain, and promised himself other summer days with her to come, and other years, when she was better – as he would make her be.

'Jenny,' he said, quietly, without meaning to speak and listening to himself. She looked up, wearily, but caught some note in his voice that interested her, 'I want so much to see you well. My home seems so large to me now. Hardly do I wish to return to it when I know that you are here. I beg of you that I may come home to you.' He took her hand, smiling and almost laughing as he found himself saying this. The sense of confidence that he had in her elated him; indeed Sim felt for a moment almost drunk by it. But, this said, he had clambered to the same height as Bagshaw and Harewood before him, so that when he turned his eyes on her he was less heady. Miss Wagstaff saw this, and a smile flickered across her mouth. She read the sudden uncertainty that had overtaken him. There came a wicked light in her eyes and, as he made a tentative enquiry of her, she almost laughed to see the doubt in him. This became the more so when the doctor became grave and seemed to think that he should stand, as he did, bending over her and holding her hands between his own. As he did this the colour rose in her face, as the gravity of what he asked occurred to her; but like a lamp placed on a window sill at night she drew him on.

'I wish that I had more to recommend me, Jenny, but I beg you to accept me. I may never attain a fortune but hope always to have funds and be able to offer you a respectable home. I promise you everything, Jenny, every good thing within my power of giving, the greatest fidelity, and lifelong friendship, if you will but consent to become my wife.'

Miss Wagstaff considered what he said and Sim, unburdened, got up and stood to his full height but placed her hands gently down before he did so. Of a sudden she raised her head but then sank back and closed her eyes, the better, in that moment, to contain herself.

'Yes,' she said, 'I should like that very much.' She opened her eyes and smiled, and the two joined hands.

Sim swallowed hard and busied himself about nothing, but could not look at her. 'I shall be very proud to be your wife,' she said. She raised herself and, finding his eyes, put a hand on each of his shoulders, turning her face to his. Sim at last looked at her. There came a moment then when the contract was sealed between them; they understood each other and, just before the discomfort of her position became too great, each rested their forehead on the other. She fell back onto the bed and, as she did so, Sim confided that he loved her. She smiled and nodded, and as she rested back on her pillow closed her eyes – but found his hand across the blanket top.

'There is something else,' he said. 'I had a child by a servant.'

Jenny opened her eyes. She was surprised at this. 'You will be faithful to me?'

'I swear it!'

She nodded wearily, and seemed already to have accommodated herself to this news. He was grateful too that she asked about the child and seemed so accepting of her and of him. 'My father has had similar liaisons,' she said. 'But you will not, not again?'

'No, Jenny,' he said. 'Not again.'

He had, for a moment, been thinking of his little girl, but the mention of the old man jolted him and Sim was frustrated that he could not go to ask for his blessing. The old man had gone into town. He had business in the city and was glad to be relieved of his burden of care. It had been a hard and anxious week for him, as for her. In other circumstances Sim would have waited for him but the doctor was late, he had a call to make, and was guilty to have put his wish to remain before the welfare of his patient. That, indeed, was the sort of thing Harewood might do. It was this thought that finally persuaded him to leave, but before he did he looked into the mingled brown and green of Jenny's eyes and promised to return as soon as he might. At the door he looked back once. She sat up and made a brave attempt at gaiety, waving a hand and smiling a wide smile: indeed, she was happy. Then the door closed behind him and she listened to the very last of his footfalls on the stairs.

154

Chapter 31

While Sim was with Jenny, Taplin, believing him to be further away, took opportunity to pry among his master's business. The other servants were busy and he slipped unseen into the doctor's study.

The room was small, lit by a window and sparely furnished. There were a desk, chair and other things, but in essence it was Spartan, and this aided Taplin in searching it.

Since Harewood had taken him into his pay Taplin had become assiduous in seeking out information. He gleaned gossip, sifting it carefully; he watched who came to the house; he watched his master; and he hunted for information, as he did now.

The room was quiet as he moved into it, although the board floor creaked under his weight. On the wall, too, a clock ticked and this added to his feeling of intrusion. Sim's presence was palpable.

Near the window, at an angle to it, was the doctor's desk , and the chair behind this represented him strongly by its broad shoulders. Taplin was rough with it, yanking it aside, but put it back again as it had been, mindful to leave no trace. He fancied himself as one who might slip like a deer among trees, although he had a more louche reputation than he imagined. One could see this shiftiness now; he had a sour face and his eyes, which

155

were normally doleful, were quick to every noise, but as he stole across the floor to the desk he had no sense of guilt; discovery would have been an inconvenience and no occasion for shame. There was money to be earned and he meant to have it.

On the desk were a number of letters, and under a large cloth was the doctor's talking machine, which Taplin had collected from Mr Wagstaff's house. The letters were mixed with case notes, and some of these were interesting to him. Among them, one in particular caught his eye. There was a man in the city, Hone, who was reasonably prosperous. Hone had ambition to be a gentleman, so Taplin despised him; thus a note in Sim's hand about a treatment to Mr Hone was intriguing: 'Prescribed a laxative, which operated within two hours of Mr Hone's return from the apothecary. Mr Hone reported several good stools, which afforded him much relief.'

Taplin laughed at this. 'Yow ay s' very different, Master Hone,' he said, showing yellowed and crooked teeth. He shuffled this sheet in among the others and moved to a second pile on the opposite side. Once again he read odd sheets. It seemed that this stack was unrewarding, but then he found something. Taplin lifted up a letter. It seemed that the doctor had expectations of getting married. He wrote to his mother requesting a ring, which, it seemed, had been passed through the family. Taplin quite thrilled to find this, as sometimes he looked and found nothing. He was encouraged, and next opened a drawer; it was there, as chance would have it, that he found something better. He took a letter and read it, tracing the lines with a finger. At length he put the letter back, and precisely covered his tracks.

Later that day Taplin had duties in the city and could meet Harewood. By now the arrangement between them was familiar; they could generally anticipate each others' movements. They had also become clever in disguising their commerce, which suited Taplin, who loved any sort of subterfuge. He was smug today as he waited in Breadmarket Street. There was a wind blowing, obliging people to keep their heads down. Consequently they might not see him, but he was very likely to see them. At the narrowest part of the street was the tower of St Mary's Church, and this was where he waited, in a recess between two buttresses. In the ordinary way Harewood would have come quickly, but today he did not. It seemed to Taplin

that the world was in motion, except for Harewood. He was
hugely frustrated. He could not wait indefinitely; some of his
work might be done by others, but much would remain for him.
Just on the point of leaving, however, Taplin saw Harewood turn
the corner, mounted on a bay horse. Harewood came on and
stopped opposite him.

'Mr Taplin. My girth appears to be loose; perhaps you
would adjust it for me?' Taplin came forward, stepped into the
road, but firstly raised one hoof of the horse's front legs.
Harewood looked down at him nervously. 'Go on, man!'

'There be tow bits o' news, Master.'

'How is Miss Wagstaff?' asked Harewood. 'Do you know?'

'No, I doh. I con foind out.'

'If you would.'

Taplin looked up to fix the terms of their present bargain.
As if swotting a fly, Harewood waved a hand, but each knew that
the transaction was sealed.

'Ah'm sorry t' tell yow, Master,' said Taplin, who turned
purposely to see the face of the doctor as he knew that he would
hurt him, 'that the doctor, Doctor Sim that be' – he dragged it
out seeing in the stiff features of Harewood that he steeled
himself – 'that there is like t' be an engagement Sir, the doctor
an' Miss Wagstaff, if yow tek me meanin', Sir.'

'What do you mean that you're sorry? What business is it of
yours? You are impertinent, Sir!' As he said this, Harewood
snatched his eyes from the blank but plainly unkind ones of his
informer. He saw the pleasure that Taplin was gaining from this.
'There were two items of news,' he snapped.

'Ah'll tek me fee, Master, thank yow, fust.'

Harewood looked disgusted, but a rummage through a
pocket produced a coin and this, first inspected by Taplin, was
satisfactory. Taplin now fiddled with the girth of the doctor's
saddle and Harewood was obliged to remove himself, a charade
that infuriated him.

'Ah'll 'ave the serme again, Sir, if yow plaese,' said Taplin.
'Yow wo' be disappointed.'

This request provoked Harewood. It was so marked that he
could hardly maintain the pretence of an everyday meeting. He
fished out a coin, however, this of greater value, and thrust it at
Taplin. 'Damn you,' he said.

'Thank yow, Sir,' said Taplin. He remained calm, enjoyed Harewood's agitation and made him wait, while Harewood grew beside himself. 'That talking' machine,' he said at last. Harewood nodded, not particularly interested. ''T' doctor's got a bet with a gentlemon that 'e con mek it say t' Lord's Prayer.'

The interview had to this point left Harewood like one of the prize fighters he sometimes treated. Another blow might have brought him to his knees; he hardly had the strength to listen. This news, though, quickened him. Goodness, how could Sim be so stupid? How, too, might he be so depraved? This was dangerous to Sim and Harewood immediately began to consider it. Taplin smiled. He had been right; it had been worth a pretty penny.

The girth was at last tightened and Taplin helped the doctor up into the saddle.

'Thank you,' said Harewood, catching Taplin's eyes a moment, 'You have done well.'

Taplin made a respectful gesture. For a moment he wanted to ask how Harewood would use the information, but the doctor forgot him. Taplin returned to work, a little resentful of the slight. He was glad that he had hurt him. Harewood, though, had not meant to slight the servant; he had simply forgotten him. Indeed, the doctor forgot his purpose in being there; many were the people who noticed him and there were some comments at his expense, but again he did not know. The busy world passed him by and he sat atop his horse until, at last, he realised that people laughed at him. By then he had come to an important conclusion. Sim must not escape the censure that he so richly deserved and if he, Harewood, were to bring this matter to light who could blame him? So he pricked his horse and moved off at a smart trot, moving into the traffic, passing the women with their baskets, the priests with their flat hats and all the many others, and turning down Bird Street, heading as fast as he could to speak with Mr Wagstaff. By luck, when he reached the house Wagstaff, just then returned, opened the door himself.

Chapter 32

Sim had had to stay overnight at his call and found work waiting for him upon his return. This kept him from Jenny, and he might have said exactly how long he had been gone. It had made him frantic to be detained, but at last he could return to her and bowled along, the sun warm, sky blue and life good, really, save her illness.

He was happy because he went to ask for her hand. He eagerly anticipated their marriage, and though she continued ill her condition gave him hope. Sim detected signs of recovery, although he did not like to mention it. Rational as he was he was still frightened to tempt fate, but she did improve. Whisper it that she would be well.

The cathedral was lit by the good light and its sandstone showed its best. The colour of the stone pleased him but it spoke to him of himself. The warmth of it was like the glow he felt in his gut. Since her acceptance of him, and her improvement, all manner of things pleased him: happiness, like an old friend, was always stealing upon him.

At one point Sim was acknowledged by a cleric who passed him on the path. He was pleased by this but smiled at the man's black clothes. By contrast he himself wore gaudy colours and a shirt with frills at the sleeves. He had a fine coat too, his breeches were fine and his stockings were silken, luxurious and the best that money could buy. All these things were symbols, outward manifestations of his youthful vigour. He felt strong and well and vital.

The march along the side of the cathedral quickly brought Mr Wagstaff's house into view, but he stopped a moment to listen to a blackbird. The bird spoke something of his feelings; it seemed to sing of him and in this mood he also halted to tease himself. It was tantalising to stop short of Jenny. The expectation of seeing her grew by the moment, and eventually he could stand it no longer. He strode up to the door but was not alone in anticipating his visit – as just inside Mr Wagstaff waited. The doctor did not know of Harewood's errand there the previous day: things were now very different.

Sim gave the door a rap and expected that Anne, a servant, would answer it, but when the door opened he was confronted not by Anne but by Mr Wagstaff. It was the work of a moment to see that the old man was changed. This was something that he imputed to some occurrence regarding Jenny: Sim felt his stomach drop. The shock was something that he would remember in the sober thought that came later. He tried to speak and managed something. 'Miss Wagstaff . . . she is not – is she worse? Tell me, please!'

He was confused because Mr Wagstaff was, in this moment, like a small and malevolent elf. He had never been handsome, and with age his face had wrinkled, his cheeks dropped and his eyes become small; but his present appearance was quite ludicrous.

'She is no worse,' muttered Wagstaff. He said this as though the reverse was true, and as Sim grew loose with relief he noticed that the expression of the old man had remained the same.

'My dear Sir,' said Sim, 'What ails you? Colic perhaps? May I assist you?'

It was not the colic, as Mr Wagstaff explained. 'You are an atheist, Sir.'

Ah, thought Sim, that would explain it. He sighed a drawn-out sigh, which he seemed to extend because he could not stomach what would come after it. He looked at the old man and, at last, spoke directly into his eyes. 'That is not strictly true, Mr Wagstaff. I am not, as you, say, strictly an atheist.'

'Not strictly a Christian either,' said Mr Wagstaff.

Sim shook his head. He was embarrassed and glanced at

160

Wagstaff, hoping to find some scope for explanation and apology. Mr Wagstaff seemed to comprehend this and there followed a moment of flux between them. In this moment Sim's mind was working. It was exasperating that he was now sorry when it would do him no good.

'There is a woman ill upstairs whom we both love,' he ventured. 'Are we not united by that and what else matters, beside the need of supporting her and making her well?'

Whether this was true or not, it made no difference. The old man did not even bother to respond to it. The doctor generally had an answer ready, but did not now know what to say as the stubborn old devil was so implacable. Sim would have liked to force his way past him. He desperately wanted to gain admittance, but eyed Mr Wagstaff with a view to persuasion and an appeal to reason. Mr Wagstaff spoke first.

'You have deceived me. You have brought sedition into my home. Your fossils, in my keeping, are evidence to you of Nature without God, are they not? But to me they show the hand of the Almighty. God within Nature, Sir, God within Nature!'

'I was too solicitous, Sir, of your good opinion. My mind, Sir.'

'Your talking machine,' Mr Wagstaff interrupted him, 'is to say the Lord's Prayer? How could you make mock of the Lord's Prayer! I am not so old or stupid that I do not realise it; you make the words meaningless by having them said by a machine. You take our faith and ridicule it. How dare you, Sir!'

'I have been stupid.' Sim meant it but his mind was racing. How was it that the man knew this? He was crestfallen. 'I have not thought as I should. You are right to upbraid me.'

'I do upbraid you!' Wagstaff was furious, his piggy eyes blazed and some motion ran through his cheeks. 'If I were a younger man I should beat you!'

'Mr Wagstaff.' Sim bent down and framed his words with his hands. The old man listened; indeed, if he had not, Sim might have raised his voice. He was terribly in earnest. 'I have not shown you or your faith the respect that you both deserve but, Sir, it was the science that cured George that has led me to think as I do. I cannot help that. If I cannot think myself into believing then pity me, Sir, but do not cast me out. I am a young man and my views are not fixed. I hope to believe. This place, the goodness of your daughter, the discovery of a spiritual sense even within me, among other things, has made me want it and I beg you to let me carry on with my life and seek for it as I may.'

'No, Sir, I will not forgive you!'

'Forgive me!' cried Sim.

'Not I,' blazed Wagstaff.

'So,' said Sim, drawing himself up to his full height, sarcastic now. 'This is the Christian charity of which I hear so much.'

Old Wagstaff was like a trout that had been wrenched from its pool. 'You have the effrontery to say that to me, Sir? I shall give you satisfaction.'

The old man threw off his nightcap and began upon his silken day coat, his brown, bony hands struggling at the buttons. Sim noticed, slowly shaking his head, the man's slender wrists, which were like twigs on a hawthorn hedge.

'That will not be necessary, Sir.'

Just then Sim thought that he heard Jenny, although he could not hear what she said, with the exception that she called his name. He shouted once, over the old man's bluster. 'Your daughter needs my care' he said.

The old man shook his head. 'Doctor Harewood has been given the care of my daughter, Sir. She is no longer any concern of yours.'

'I assure you, Sir, that she is.' Despite his restraint Sim stepped closer to the old man.

'I am aware, Sir,' hissed Wagstaff, 'that you have seduced my daughter's good opinion but you will not be permitted to have any further contact with her. You will not marry her, Sir, nor will she ever again give you more than "good day", and now you will leave my property. I pay you no compliments and cannot wish you even so much as "good afternoon". Goodbye, Sir!'

The doctor had taken a step forwards as the old man placed a hand on the door. Just at the last he thought that he heard Jenny again, but then the door slammed shut in his face.

Sim could not afterward account for the next few minutes. When he next became aware of the time his watch had advanced; he had wandered some little way off but had no memory of it. When at last he became collected he was mortified that he could not see Jenny. Without exaggeration he might have wept. She needed him, too. Heaven save her from Harewood! He removed his wig and carried it home, almost as if it were a favourite cat killed by a carriage that he meant to bury, dragging his feet until, somewhere near to the cathedral's west front, he realised where the information about the machine had come from; and thereafter his pace quickened markedly.

Chapter 33

'Taplin! Taplin!' The doctor clattered through his house, throwing doors open as he went. One of the other servants showed herself. He waved a hand. 'Taplin!'

Momentarily he stopped, on the landing, halfway up the stairs. His big frame was silhouetted against a window while he listened. A door opened behind him: it was another servant. He threw his wig at her and began upon the upper staircase. 'Taplin!'

There were few rooms in the house and Sim would find him soon. It was better that he showed himself and someone, in malice, told Taplin this. Seeing it to be true, and the dislike of the other servants toward him, he stepped into the hall but banged the door in the faces of those behind him. He shut them out, but they opened it again and, overhead, Sim heard the noise of it. He stopped on the second staircase, looked down and there was Taplin. Sim bounced down the steps two at a time until the two men stood face to face.

'Yes, Master?' Taplin was civil enough, except that his posture, tone and manner said something else. He had hardly ever looked Sim in the eye before but he did so now.

'I should beat you,' said Sim. 'You gave details of a wager that I made to Doctor Harewood.'

'Ah day,' said Taplin.

'Do you know,' snapped Sim, 'what has come of this? Who knows where it may end?'

'I day do it.'

'You did.'

Taplin shrugged. 'Ah never. Ah told yow.'

The doctor turned away in disgust. 'What a fool I have been with you. But no more. I give you a quarter of an hour to leave my home. I dismiss you. You may go where they will have you or starve and if you are not gone in fifteen minutes I shall throw you out.'

'Am yow man enough to do that, Master?' said Taplin. There was no mistaking this. 'When boys play at bein' men they get hurt.'

'Fifteen minutes,' said Sim. 'If you are not gone by then I shall remove you, and you may apply to Doctor Harewood for medical attention.'

The doctor stomped away up the stairs, and thus it was that twenty minutes later Doctor Harewood was treated to a diverting spectacle. The doctor was standing in the window of an upstairs room when, by chance, he noticed a commotion in the road. Like a navvy, Sim brawled with his servant! The doctor, with his practised eye, measured weight against weight, reach and height, and hoped that Taplin might humiliate Sim, or that Sim would hurt Taplin for that matter. At best, perhaps they might seriously injure each other? He could but hope. For this reason he was irritated by three do-gooders who tried to stop the fight. It went on, however, and the men rolled in the muck of the gutter. If only, thought Harewood, Sim's apologists might see him now! He began to think of watching from the road, but then Sim bent Taplin double. From his knees Taplin sank onto his face. 'Get up!' willed Harewood, but Taplin was beaten. 'Coward!' shouted Harewood. 'Coward!' He was so close to the glass as he shouted this that the window fogged.

Across the road Sim stood over his opponent, and when he saw that Taplin wanted no more turned, marched into his house and slammed his door behind him.

'Do not answer the door!' shouted Harewood. He was wise in saying this. After about a minute Taplin got up and came towards his house. 'Do not answer it!'

Taplin knocked. He knocked once, twice, three times, and finally belaboured the door. No-one stirred. Finally he moved off, but the doctor wanted to repay him. He had many grievances against Taplin, and for this reason he allowed Taplin to see him. For a moment Taplin made some sort of appeal to him, and Harewood had the satisfaction of ignoring him. The two men were joined by their mutual dislike. Then Taplin wandered off, not before cursing Harewood; but Harewood smiled a thin smile. He continued to watch until Taplin had gone, and he enjoyed doing it.

So it was that Harewood was more than satisfied as he returned to his chair. It seemed, as they say, that he had killed two birds with one stone. Admittedly it was a nasty business, but who might blame him? Taplin was not worth a second thought and Sim had stolen so much from him. Of the two, was not Sim even worse than Taplin? He brought sedition, but Harewood was not proud of what he had done. Here again, however, he showed superiority. He had principle and conscience enough to regret what had been forced upon him; it was the want of principle and conscience in Sim that was most truly culpable.

At length he got up and looked again through the window. Over the way he could see the cathedral, behind which was the house where Miss Wagstaff lay ill. She would need him now. At last she would see him for what he was. Her life was in his hands. He would heal her, and be vindicated.

Chapter 34

6 'I will not take it. I desire Doctor Sim to attend me. Go away!' Miss Wagstaff rolled her head and refused Harewood's medicine. The doctor, perched on the bed, concentrated upon his laden spoon and tried to keep his temper. It was politic to do this as he was thoroughly insulted: how dare she ask for Sim. But he had a reputation to uphold, and once placed a hand on the rear of her neck. Briefly he looked across at her father.

'I fear that the distemper, Sir, is settling in her brain.'

'How dare you!' said his patient. 'You are the blockhead.'

'Blockhead!' Mr Wagstaff jumped up.

'Blockhead,' she repeated.

'Blockhead or not,' said Mr Wagstaff, his piggy eyes blinking repeatedly, 'he will treat you!' The old man gave a nod to the doctor. 'Go to, Sir. Go to.'

Harewood was for a moment distracted from his duty, and the old man found himself the object of the doctor's grey eyes. The doctor seemed on the point of some observation.

'Go to, Sir,' said Mr Wagstaff. 'She will be made to accept you.'

'I fear, Mr Wagstaff,' said Harewood, letting out a rather tired sigh, 'that I can do no more now.' He rose from the bed, reaching to a chair under the window where his coat lay draped. 'But I *will* return.' He said this in a very pointed manner. Harewood was nothing if not stubborn. 'I shall return this

167

evening after you have had opportunity of talking to your daughter. I bid you good day, Madam; Sir.'

'I wonder if you would do me a service, Sir,' said Miss Wagstaff. She raised her head and looked at him.

'Aye, Madam, gladly,' replied Harewood. 'What may that be?'

'Send me Doctor Maximum. Doctor Minimum is of no consequence to me.'

Harewood took up his bag and stomped out as though his breeches were too tight. The door, with a thud, closed behind them. The sudden privacy, once they were gone, was like coming upon shade on a hot afternoon. It had been a trying encounter and she was glad to sink back, but listened to her breathing. This, increasingly, had a morbid fascination for her; she knew that she was weaker. If only she might have continued with Sim.

She wondered where her doctor was and looked at the chair where he had sat beside her only a day or so since. Suddenly the door opened. She steeled herself, expecting her father's rancour, but it was not her father. Jenny smiled in relief and affection at Anne, the house servant. Anne had a face like a harvest moon, round and good natured, and she brought a message.

'The doctor, Ma'am, Doctor Sim, he wanted me to speak to you.'

Miss Wagstaff eased herself up and some colour came into her face. A flicker of laughter passed between them and Anne sat down. She tried to recall Sim's words, and there was something of his voice in what she said that brought him close for Jenny.

'The doctor asks your pardon, Ma'am. He was wrong to accept the wager and begs you to forgive him.' Jenny nodded. Anne glanced at the door and became breathless. 'He also wonders if you would consent to an elopement.'

The colour rose in Jenny's face and, unconsciously, she took up Anne's hands, saying that she would. The two women laughed. Some of the bloom even returned to Jenny, and for a moment she was bright and animated. 'Yes!' she said. 'Please be good enough to tell him that I shall.'

Anne glanced at the door and raised a hand. She had to be quick. Jenny prepared to listen. 'The doctor begs you to eat well and do everything that Doctor Harewood asks of you, so that you will be well enough to travel.'

Jenny nodded and was a little breathless. She began to say

168

something, but then they heard the footsteps of Mr Wagstaff. 'We must go soon,' she said.

Anne nodded and sprang from the bed. Jenny indicated the bedclothes and Anne bent to tuck the blankets in. Barely had she begun before her master came in. Mr Wagstaff was ill-natured. Unlike him, as it was, he pointed to the door. Anne dropped into a curtsey and the door closed behind her.

'How dare you, Madam!' This was the sort of anger that she had learned to dread in childhood. 'You forget yourself!' Mr Wagstaff's pig eyes were white rimmed and his cheeks shook. 'You see how you anger me?'

He swallowed and moved about, the breath rattling in him, but then he did something unexpected; he dropped down beside the bed. To this point she had refused to look at him; now she was induced to look, but he was no longer angry. To tell the truth, the old man looked old, worn and desperate. Suddenly she was glad to give her hands. She knew his devotion to her: her father would have taken her place without a second thought.

'Jenny, he is a bad man. You must forget him. I beg you too, for my sake, that you must get well. I beg you! When the doctor calls again, please will you co-operate?'

The appeal that he made of her was so earnest. Its sincerity upset her, especially as she was to deceive him. She cried a little but her father, colouring, made light of it, fussing to find a handkerchief about him. She smiled in taking the handkerchief, in embarrassment, but this smile, which was dear to him, set him off fidgeting again. As he reddened and shuffled she smiled again, but this time at him. He had such strong feelings and so much difficulty in showing them. She was embarrassed too, however, and could not look at him for long. She was troubled because she hated to deceive him. He had always been true and had instilled the same thing in her, but her life had taken this turn and she loved Sim, whose society, for all his wrong regarding his machine, was necessary to her.

'I love you, Papa,' she said, and for a moment cared for nothing except that his pig eyes took her meaning. As they did so the old man struggled with himself. He found it easier to show his love than tell it, but she knew this.

'I shall co-operate with the doctor,' she said.

'I thank you!' The old man rolled in his chair as he

swallowed his relief, rubbing her hand with his. 'Thank you! Good girl! Good girl! Now rest, rest and get well.'

He bent over stiffly, kissed her and then padded to the door where, typically, he nodded in lieu of something more emotional. She smiled at this and then, very softly, he closed the door behind him. Soon afterward Anne took his place.

Chapter 35

Once Sim heard that Miss Wagstaff would elope his mood lifted, and all his natural optimism and energy came into play. However, he would not gather Jenny up and go without thought or hindrance. His patients needed a physician, and nor did he wish them to fall into Harewood's care. Fortunately he had a friend, Doctor Ruddock, who was free to come and act as locum, and so this arrangement was speedily made.

In making his plans Sim was fortunate in having several friends; many a person would have done him a service and kept it secret. Sadly, though, he was loath to trust anyone, but as Ruddock was unknown Sim entrusted him, and miles from Lichfield he bought Sim's ring.

Some of the doctor's problems were more intractable; but in each case they endorsed his view that every problem has its solution. For example: the matter of transport. Sim was troubled how to remove Jenny, but one of his own carriages proved to be suitable, one which, with little alteration, would permit an occupant to lie down. Thus it would be possible to cover great distances, such as the road to Scotland – where the marriage was to be sealed.

When last he had heard of Jenny she had been complying with the instructions of Doctor Harewood. Sim was glad of this; he was also pleased that Mr Wagstaff remained in ignorance of the plan. The old man might easily have come upon it. Nor had Anne been compromised. This was important to Sim. In the face of every difficulty they had settled upon a date. He and Jenny would leave upon the night, forthcoming, of the full moon. Moonlight would make it possible to travel by night; it would also encourage Mr Wagstaff to visit a friend in Walsall. Sim was confident that they would be gone when the old man came home, and more than that they must trust to chance.

When everything had been done there came a time when all that remained was to wait. This was the hard part of the plan. The days dragged; Sim could hardly attend his work. In fact he became rather abstracted. One potentially lucrative malady (bubbles before the eyes) was met with the offhand recommendation that the patient should not look at them. At this she had been taken elsewhere.

For all this, though, the moment arrived. Upon rising that morning a thrill ran through Sim: this was the day; in this period of wakefulness the wheels would turn under them. He only had to get through a few more hours and, in consequence, was thankful of things that occupied him. Around lunchtime Doctor Ruddock arrived and thereafter Sim suffered the guilt of not being at home to people who called for him.

In closing his doors to the outside he was left with the problem of his own household. They sensed that something extraordinary was coming to a head. He noticed that they probed him; he became subjected to back-handed questions, which was natural but impertinent. In consequence, he retired to a private quarter but, once he had done this, realised something. It became obvious that he should have worked until the last moment. A feeling of agitation grew in him steadily until he thought of nothing except the hall clock. This became so severe that eventually he strode about in the quarter hours. Downstairs the servants looked up and listened to him as he moved about.

In this way the sense of agitation in the house was not confined to Sim; so much so that they waited for the time when he would move. They guessed that this would come with the dusk and so it was. Upstairs the long-awaited moment almost seemed to topple him. His nerves jangled like pots and pans carried by a tinker. None the less, he collected himself, breathed deeply and took to the stairs. Before he reached the hall, all his resolution and excitement had returned to him. However, he then realised that he had to say something to his servants. He hated lies, but explained that he was to go and stay with his mother. He told them this and saw that none believed him. Indeed, there was a moment of flux; they knew and he knew this. One or two of his servants almost stepped outside the role allotted them. The senior servant said that he wished the doctor well and a safe and successful journey, something Sim might have resented but perhaps not. He saw that they were well wishing and, in a moment of candour and gratitude, almost told them the truth.

So it was that the horses were put in the traces and all the servants, it seemed, were on hand to see him go. The doctor turned his eyes on them, then stepped into the dusk and the door was shut behind him.

From the moment that he left the house the plan became active. He had carried on a correspondence with Anne and it was settled where he would wait. All had been so dangerous for her, however, that he had seldom dared to contact her. There were so many spies as Taplin had proved. Despite this, he knew when Mr Wagstaff was expected to leave, by what means and in which direction he would go. Thus Sim took himself to Minster Pool where he would wait his time.

In the daytime the walk beside the pool was a place where people might admire the cathedral across the water. In the dark it lost its appeal, and as Sim had expected it was deserted. The path was overhung with trees and Sim was able to hide, while still being able to see the road.

The doctor's nerves were now tightly drawn and to extend the time of waiting might have seemed foolish. This being so, he had taken the precaution of being early. He needed to be sure that Mr Wagstaff had not already left. At first he waited cheerfully; but as one minute followed another, and the time elapsed when Wagstaff should have left, he became less happy. The doctor shifted his weight and began to mutter under his breath until, eventually, he started to talk to himself. His agitation became so great that finally he was forced to seek distraction. Such was the beauty of a birdsong that he found a measure of relief; the black shape of a bird piped a song, and he stared at this with a childish wonder. When he moved and frightened the bird he was pained to lose its company. He was at a loss for a little while how to contain his feelings but forced himself to take an interest in the houses upon the far bank. Sim looked at these as he had never done so before. He was fascinated how their lines began to blur with the evening until, as the light died, they became house shapes. He was drawn to the light of their windows, which began to glow and wink, and over them how the roofs were sharply defined as the blue above them turned black. He waited and continued to wait, until a carriage appeared and Sim, jolted, recognised it as that belonging to Mr Wagstaff.

The path of the carriage led along the road that ran before the head of the Pool. It showed a lamp in the dark and some of the noise of the wheels reached Sim and the jangle and rattle of the thing as it passed by.

Sim was obliged to wait a moment or so in order to compose himself. It did not do for a gentleman to have no self possession. The anticipation of this moment was, however, quite wonderful. The road was open for them and he now watched for Jenny. Hardly had he waited two or three minutes more before a figure appeared, just at the point where the Close met Dam Street and the road went on to pass right and left around the cathedral.

It was, of course, now dark and Sim was elated that all went so well. No-one had come upon him, nor was there anyone to gawp or interfere. He showed himself, gave the signal and went bowling forward. His intention was to take Jenny up and kiss her, something which was not remotely proper, but what of it? They would be married within two or three days and none would come between them. It was, however, Anne who came to meet him.

'My mistress is mighty unwell, Sir. She cannot come. She begs you to forgive her.'

Among the various emotions of this moment one was annoyance, but this was only one among a number. He swiftly begged her pardon and she was good to him as he put his hands to his face. For the moment, poor Sim was quite at a loss. Anne came near him: her big, round face was leaden and she behaved as if the fault was hers. She and the doctor looked at each other.

'Pardon me,' said Sim, 'and please tell your mistress that of course I forgive her but I shall go myself and tell her.'

'No, Sir. The master, Sir. He's still at home. The carriage you saw was Brown gone to get Doctor Harewood. You must go home, Sir. Another time, perhaps.'

Sim was appalled. His frustration at the old man almost overcame him: he cursed to tell the truth, but he apologised and, while he had Anne with him, began to tax her. He had question upon question for her but she raised a hand. She had taken great risk in leaving the house and might be missed at any time. She had to go back. Sim, nodding, was good enough to remember her needs as well as his own. He excused her and gave her a coin before she ran away, hitching her skirts up as she went, and once again he was left to himself in the dark.

The doctor had no choice; he must go home. But before he did so he walked into the Close and, in the shadow of the cathedral, deep in the angle of a buttress, just where the building turned like a ship's stern at its end, he stood and looked at Mr Wagstaff's home. It was a misery to him to be excluded but he hoped in Harewood, as chance and irony would have it.

Before long that gentleman appeared and quite ran into the house. The door opened for him and closed behind him and Sim wandered home, stumbling in a minute or two later like a ghost. 'It has misfired,' he said, without pretence. His servants were almost friends to him now and he was glad of them. One went, without being asked, to find the horses. The others wanted to discuss the misadventure and console him, but this was not possible. The door was shut and he was still in the drawing room when Ruddock came home, hours later. Ruddock was shocked to see that Sim was red about the eyes, and had he not known better might have thought that he had been crying.

Chapter 36

Sim sat some while after Doctor Ruddock had gone to bed, and it was growing light before he climbed the stairs. He arose soon after Ruddock, although kept to himself and said or did no more than was necessary. However, he stirred himself to gather various things in a bag, chief among these being the medicine with which he had been treating Jenny. Sim had some idea that he might yet be called upon. For this reason, once he had shaved and dressed and eaten a morsel he waited upstairs, the servants knowing where he might be found.

The call, though, did not come. The day bloomed into a bright morning and into a fine afternoon. Sim's house was blessed with a number of windows and these allowed a flood of light in, particularly the window, in its round arch, that lit the stairway halfway up. The light was so bright and so unremittingly cheerful that even Sim could not be blind to it, and it coaxed him into a more optimistic way of thinking. Indeed he strayed so far as the garden at the front of the house. For a moment or two, while he was there, he almost forgot.

The doctor waited, but the only person to call was Doctor Ruddock – whom Sim, now a little restored, was pleased to see. Somewhat embarrassed by the previous night, he made some effort to entertain him and the two friends ate a good meal. They were each of an easy character and their friendship, too, made it possible for talk to come readily, once the servants had

176

withdrawn, although Sim was not himself. Ruddock, however, compensated for this. He was enjoying his work and keen to discuss it. There were already one or two eccentrics with whom he had become acquainted, and some of the amusements and the rigours of the working day were rich pickings for him.

Sim kept a good cellar and some wine was brought out, but Sim would only sip his. In truth he only pretended to do this, but Doctor Ruddock did not seem to notice it. Ruddock drank, although did not forget that he might yet be called upon; but they were easy, easy as they might be. One man sat slumped in one fireside chair and the other slumped opposite, their legs stretched out so that their feet almost met. In the grate the doctor would have a fire once it was dark, by the leave of his guest, because he enjoyed the orange quality of the light. Sim found that he might think in looking into the flames and hoped that Ruddock would realise when he wished for privacy.

Presently their conversation lapsed, and perhaps Sim was lost in some reverie as he failed to hear a summons at the door, which Ruddock was obliged to bring to his attention. At last, however, Sim jumped up, suddenly shocked and disjointed, as a servant told him something that he found hard to understand.

'Doctor Harewood, Sir, Doctor Harewood wishes to speak with you urgently.'

Ruddock got to his feet, although he did so in a manner that was calculated not to increase the evident alarm. For a moment he enquired of Sim whether he should leave. He did this without speaking, but Sim waved him to sit and, composing himself, stood to his full height. Harewood came in. Thus the two arch-enemies were joined, and much was said without a word being spoken.

'The transfusion,' said Harewood at last, as Ruddock moved to offer a chair, 'has misfired. Miss Wagstaff is now very weak.' He cast his eyes between them. He looked exhausted. 'She is desperately ill, Sim. Will you come? I need your help. I beg you to come.'

Doctor Sim stood now like a straw man, and it seemed that he had trouble understanding the import of what was said to him. For what seemed like an unending moment he stared, rather stupidly, into the grate and thereafter, foolishly, looked for his wig, which he had removed. Harewood stood and watched him, limp and defeated. It was Doctor Ruddock who found the wig. Sim tried to fit it but then threw it aside.

'She is still alive?' he asked.

'She is still alive,' Harewood replied.

Sim remembered his bag, his bag full of miraculous cures, which had in truth snatched people before now from the gates of death, and picked it up. When this was done they raced through the house, their shoes scraped on the tiles and the door banged behind them. Doctor Ruddock, and some of the servants who had been disturbed, came out to watch them go, and the two doctors were quickly away.

It was, of course, the work but of a couple of minutes, a little more or a little less, before the doctors reached the foot of the stairs that would take them up to Jenny, and at this point came a moment for consideration. They knew that they should not blunder into the room as if joined at one leg, so they stopped, just for a moment. Now was time to acquire composure and, belatedly, co-operate. Harewood told Sim what had been administered and Sim nodded. The doctor whispered and Sim looked straight into his eyes, so that they looked like lovers, standing as they were cramped in the space at the bottom of the stairs. It would have been easier to remain but the one, suddenly, nodded to the other. There was something said before their ascent and then they went up.

At the top they reached a white panelled door that led off to the right from a landing. On the left were other rooms and the stairs curled on after a steep turn. On the red carpet was a table and on this a bust. Everything was well lit and ordinary, although on the other side of the door a drama was unfolding. Sim steeled himself, entered, and was shocked at finding himself, in that moment, at the centre of a stage. He saw that he had an audience that had been waiting for him. His eyes glanced off those of Mr Wagstaff, but he saw how the old man pinned his hopes on him. Even in Harewood, who had come in and taken station behind Mr Wagstaff, he saw the same thing.

Strangely the curtains had been drawn in the small, crowded room and the daylight, which had begun to fade, filtered through the curtains, giving a strange light to the proceedings: it borrowed something from the colour of the yellow summer cloth.

'Jenny!' Sim dropped onto one knee and she looked at him. In this moment he was completely forgetful of the others; it was a very private moment. Sim took her hand and she looked up at him and smiled; a good natured smile, made partly with her eyes, but her cheeks cupped and turned the corners of her mouth, just as if she had been well. Her fingers knitted with his.

'I knew that you would come. I wish we might have got away,' she said softly, shifting, trying to move in the bed. 'I would now be your wife.'

'But I shall make you well,' replied Sim. He grew perky and gave her hand a pat before he fiddled, somewhat frantically, with the catches on his bag. He smiled at her as he struggled.

'Please,' she said, with a strange sort of note in her voice, a slight movement running through her, 'open the curtains so I may see the daylight again before I die.'

Her father, Harewood and Sim, who was trying hard to collect his thoughts but whose mind would not come to heel, were united by this; they all scoffed that she was dying, but Harewood was quick to oblige for all that, the more quickly because her voice was becoming rather faint. Immediately there was a flood of the most cheerful light into the room. Mr Wagstaff took up her hand and almost pulled on it. In this some strength seemed to leave him. He had, of course, entertained a hope in Sim. Old Mr Wagstaff was deeply attached to his children; it had been more than he could do to give her up. Now, however, he was defeated and the old man cried. He sobbed, but Sim was cheerful and produced his medicine with a flourish.

'No, Jenny, what is this? I have here the very thing. This will make you well. Think of all the summer days we have in store for us; our own home, our children. Come, Jenny.' He took up some water, grabbed a glass from his bag and made some mixture, very imperfectly, and thereafter made as if he would lift her head. Sim's hand shook. 'The very thing,' he said, but the doctor's voice broke.

'I am dying,' she said, as if to herself, quietly, so much so that they hardly heard her, but they all did for all her soft words; and poor Jenny cried a little, breathing with some difficulty now, and the more so, of course, as she cried. She did not sob, but cried almost silently, with tears at intervals running on her cheeks.

Sim took up a handkerchief and wiped the water from her face, gently. He was soothing and remained busy. He had drawn up a chair and wanted her to take the medicine, but she held onto her father and sought out his hand.

'Too late,' Jenny said. She turned from the medicine. 'Hold my hand. Do not be cross with Papa.' Sim now cried a little himself. He had not done this before another person for years, but he cried now, caring nothing for his dignity. Jenny smiled when she saw him cry and made as if she would dry his tears, trying to take the handkerchief from him, but she could not. She breathed quietly that she loved her father and then looked up at Sim, lifting her eyes to look up over her fine, handsome, black brows, which were so dark and painted with so fine a hand, and smiled, a smile that turned her cheeks and shone most markedly in her eyes. As she tried to say something of her love for him, her hands grew still in that of the doctor and Mr Wagstaff; and she had left them.

Chapter 37

The bells were ringing in the cathedral as Sim looked over the pricked ears of his horse, and for a moment he turned. He had not meant to look back but, in weakness, did so. He twisted in the saddle and fiddled with the catch of the saddlebag. This, though, was a device, and he looked at his home, as it had been, which he had now given up. The house was a fine, handsome house; he felt a sort of attachment to it and had to remind himself that he would not be coming back. Down the road that led to the cathedral birds, crows, were sailing around the spires, and he was moved to see the lovely west front. He enjoyed the spires a final time, but thought of Jenny who lay buried in the cathedral, beside her mother, in a family space beneath the lady chapel.

Tears rose in his eyes and, to his shame, a stab of bitterness pierced him. He thought of Jenny's funeral. On the one hand had been the misery and on the other the happiness of Bagshaw and Mary, which, for all the grief, they had struggled to keep to themselves. He was to attend their wedding in a short while. Sim was bleak and felt that he had left himself in the lady chapel. He felt that it was a shell he took on from there. He had no anticipation of ever again belonging and his future seemed as though behind him.

It was a shame for Sim that he did not know life would seek him out. Happiness would come to his door, but he did not

189

know it. For a moment he tried almost to divine something of Jenny, as he often did nowadays, and had anyone spoken to him while he remained in the road he would not have heard them.

Thus it was that Doctor Harewood became, once again, the city's only doctor. (This is to say Lichfield's only physician; there were always quacks and practitioners of a lower standing.) This would have pleased him once, but Harewood was not the man he was and cared little whether Sim stayed or went; he had even dropped his action against him. Harewood could not forget Jenny's death either, and was haunted by the thought that he had hastened it. He had confessed this to Sim, almost hoping that Sim would humiliate him, but he would not.

So it was that they were reconciled, in some way, and Sim had also made peace with Mr Wagstaff. At the funeral the old man's grief had touched him deeply, to such an extent that he had put aside his feelings towards him. Strangely, in doing this he had found greater peace himself. He had thought it proper to apologise to Mr Wagstaff. Sim knew that he had wronged him and acted badly regarding the talking machine. He had deceived him, too, regarding the fossils and so, belatedly, had acquired greater principle and less arrogance. He supposed that this might help him in the future, even if it were too late now. He could not bring himself to say goodbye to either man, though, and would slip away.

Indeed, as Sim delayed he began to worry that someone would come upon him, and he wanted to avoid this at all costs. The doctor gently pricked his horse, the animal began a trot and Sim, looking neither left nor right, kept going until Lichfield was gone behind him.

Printed in the United Kingdom
by Lightning Source UK Ltd.
135344UK00001B/148-198/P

9 781904 408437